THRONE OF YORK

CHARLOTTE BYRD

Proofreaders:

Renee Waring, Guarding, Guardian Proofreading Services, https://www.facebook.com/GuardianProofreadingServices

Julie Deaton, Deaton Author Services, https://www.facebook.com/jdproofs/

Cover Design: Charlotte Byrd

Visit my website at www.charlotte-byrd.com

Created with Vellum

ABOUT THRONE OF YORK

I don't know who to believe, but I know that this place is full of lies and secrets.

Easton Bay has risked everything to protect me, but that doesn't mean that he didn't do what they had accused him of.

I am in love with him. **I am supposed to be his wife, but this changes everything.** The King has turned on him. I'm Easton's only hope.

But it's only a matter of time before they turn on me, too.

Is my fate is sealed?

Throne of York is the third book in the House of York Trilogy. It begins with House of York and continues with Crown of York, all available for purchase now.

In addition to Throne of York, I've included a sneak peak of my next book, *Tangled up in Ice*. You will not want to miss the dark, recluse billionaire who has consumed me!

Tangled up in Ice releases on Feb 14, 2019. **ONE-CLICK here to preorder it NOW!**

PRAISE FOR CHARLOTTE BYRD

“Decadent, delicious, & dangerously addictive!” - Amazon Review ★★★★★

“Titillation so masterfully woven, no reader can resist its pull. A MUST-BUY!” - Bobbi Koe, Amazon Review ★★★★★

“Captivating!” - Crystal Jones, Amazon Review ★★★★★

"Exciting, intense, sensual” - Rock, Amazon Reviewer ★★★★★

“Sexy, secretive, pulsating chemistry…” - Mrs. K, Amazon Reviewer ★★★★★

“Charlotte Byrd is a brilliant writer. I've read loads and I've laughed and cried. She writes a balanced book with brilliant characters. Well done!” -Amazon Review ★★★★★

“Fast-paced, dark, addictive, and compelling” - Amazon Reviewer ★★★★★

“Hot, steamy, and a great storyline.” - Christine Reese ★★★★★

“My oh my....Charlotte has made me a fan for life.” - JJ, Amazon Reviewer ★★★★★

"The tension and chemistry is at five alarm level.” - Sharon, Amazon reviewer ★★★★★

“Hot, sexy, intriguing journey of Elli and Mr. Aiden Black. - Robin Langelier ★★★★★

“Wow. Just wow. Charlotte Byrd leaves me speechless and humble... It definitely kept me on the edge of my seat. Once you pick it up, you won't put it down.” - Amazon Review ★★★★★

“Sexy, steamy and captivating!” - Charmaine, Amazon Reviewer ★★★★★

“ Intrigue, lust, and great characters...what more could you ask for?!” - Dragonfly Lady ★★★★★

“An awesome book. Extremely entertaining, captivating and interesting sexy read. I could not put it down.” - Kim F, Amazon Reviewer ★★★★★

“Just the absolute best story. Everything I like to read about and more. Such a great story I will read again and again. A keeper!!” - Wendy Ballard ★★★★★

“It had the perfect amount of twists and turns. I instantaneously bonded with the heroine and of course Mr. Black. YUM. It's sexy, it's sassy, it's steamy. It's everything.” - Khardine Gray, Bestselling Romance Author ★★★★★

HOUSE OF YORK TRILOGY

1. House of York
2. Crown of York
3. Throne of York

DON'T MISS OUT!

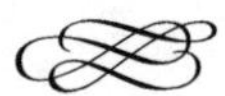

Want to be the first to know about my upcoming sales, new releases and exclusive giveaways?

Sign up for my Newsletter and join my Reader Club!

Bonus Points: Follow me on BookBub!

ALSO BY CHARLOTTE BYRD

All books are available at ALL major retailers! If you can't find it, please email me at charlotte@charlotte-byrd.com

Black Series:

Black Edge

Black Rules

Black Bounds

Black Contract

Black Limit

House of York Trilogy:

House of York

Crown of York

Throne of York

Standalone Novels:

Debt

Offer

Unknown

Dressing Mr. Dalton

PART ONE

CHAPTER 1 - EASTON

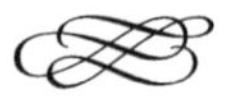

WHEN I FIRST SEE EVERLY...

I've been watching her.

I saw her name on the list.

There were others, too, but she stood out.

I've never done this before. I never sought out one of the women, let alone approached her.

I pretended that everything that happens here on this forsaken island wasn't my business.

I thought that if I didn't get involved, then it wouldn't be my fault. But that's not how life works, is it?

You are involved, all of the time.

You make decisions about your values all the time.

What you do or don't do.

What you buy or don't buy.

I tried to wash the guilt away. I tried to close my eyes to all the horrors that take place around me.

Even after they took Alicia away from me.

I thought I was in love with her and I wanted to run away with her. Yet, when they took her away from me, I believed them.

I closed my eyes to all the anger, and the hatred, and everything that I knew deep inside of myself to be true.

I closed my eyes to the truth that I felt deep inside of me.

You know that feeling that makes your skin crawl when something bad is about to happen?

You know those little goose bumps you get when you feel like something just isn't right?

You know that voice in the back of your head that tries to warn you, no matter how nice everything seems to be?

Those are signs you shouldn't ignore. But I did.

I experienced them.

I lived them.

And they became my mistakes.

Standing here, watching this room full of people talking, laughing, mingling, I realize what I knew all along.

I didn't need to overhear my father talking to his

closest advisor to confirm the truth. That nauseous feeling, those goose bumps down my arms, that sickening feeling in the back of my throat - those were all proof of it.

My father had Alicia killed, and I was too stupid, no, too naive, not to see it.

Is that why I'm here in this room with drapery around the walls and everyone dressed in their black tie best? Perhaps.

I'm here to find her.

Everly March.

I saw her name on the list and something drew me to her.

Her first name, flowing and never-ending, reminds me of a river or a rushing brook.

But her last?

Quick and strong and powerful.

It's almost as if it brings the flowing water to a sudden stop.

Everly March.

Everly March.

Everly March.

I say her name over and over again. Who are you? And why did you bring me here?

I scan the room in search of her and it doesn't

take me long. I walk by people, leaning in and listening until I hear her name.

I stand a little bit away from her, just enough so that I don't come off as a creep. And I watch and wait until her date leaves her side.

I finish a drink and get another. I continue to wait.

It is these moments that I return to over and over again, when we are apart.

The shine of her hair.

The snugness of her dress around her hips.

The way she scrunched her shoulders down, either out of shyness, or anxiety, or just to stay warm.

Her high cheekbones and large bright eyes make her face radiate and I find myself drawn to her.

It takes everything in my power to keep my distance. It's not that I want her, which I do, but it's more that I want to meet her.

Her beauty is effortless, and I immediately feel the pull of attraction.

But the pull is more than that.

It's like there's a gravitational pull around her.

She is the sun and she's drawing me to her.

When I can't stand not being close to her any longer, her date finally leaves.

There's my opening, my chance.

I approach her carefully, not because I'm afraid of spooking her, but I'm afraid of what that would do to me.

"Hello, there," I say softly from behind.

I see her considering one of the options from the silent auction.

The one she's looking at is offered by a family friend of my father's.

"Considering bidding on that yachting weekend in Newport?" I ask.

She turns around and examines me carefully. Her eyes narrow, then relax, and then she gives me a smile.

"Yes, that's right," she says with a tinge of sarcasm. "The highest bid is probably around $100,000. So, I'd have to work two and a half years at my current job and save every penny just to match it."

Of all the ways I'd thought this conversation could've possibly gone, this was not it.

I don't know who I expected to get, but this woman with a strong wit and a sharp tongue was not it.

Her reaction amuses me; it draws me in even more.

I can't help but give her a wink.

"I'm Easton," I say, holding out my hand and waiting for the moment when she will finally let me touch her.

The moment is all too brief, unfortunately.

Before I even have a chance to say another word, her date comes back. It's as if he was waiting, watching.

He wraps his arm firmly around her waist.

She is mine, his body language says. Stay away. Keep away. Get the fuck away.

I look at him and watch as his nostrils flare out.

His eyebrows furrow, his jealousy is about to be pushed over the edge.

I see him getting closer to that edge and I want to push him over it.

I want her to see the coward that he really is.

I want her to see that this isn't the good kind of possessiveness, the kind that makes a woman feel wanted. No, he is all weakness and he knows it.

"Easton, this is my…friend…Jamie."

She pauses in the middle, considering just the right description for what he is.

She does not use the word date, but friend.

This does not go unnoticed.

CHAPTER 2 - EASTON

WHEN I TRY TO WARN HER...

"Actually, she's my date," Jamie corrects her.

I raise my eyebrow in a show of acknowledgment.

He's trying to rattle me.

Trying to shock me.

Trying to throw me off kilter.

I'm not going to give in.

"I was just talking to Everly about the silent auctions here. What will you be bidding on?" I ask.

He takes a deep breath for a moment of consideration.

He's not going to bid on anything.

He doesn't have the money, but there's no way he would ever admit it.

We stare at each other for a moment, without saying a word.

"I think I'm going to go for this weekend trip to Paris," I say in the most smug and entitled way possible.

I pick up the pen and fill out the form next to the package.

"It's all for a good cause, right?" I mumble under my breath.

"It's supposed to be a silent auction," Jamie says, pulling Everly closer to him.

She shudders a little bit at how forceful he is, and I clench my jaw.

I want to punch him in his face, but that's not a wise decision.

Everly knows nothing about me.

I need her to trust me.

I'm not going to get anywhere with her if I knock out her conniving, lying, asshole of a date.

"Yes, of course. But I doubt that the foundation will be against a little competition. Especially, if that makes the bid go higher."

When he doesn't respond, I turn toward him and hand him my pen.

"Go ahead, kid," I say, squaring my shoulders with him.

I cross my arms across my chest, narrowing my eyes.

"Don't call me kid," he says, grabbing the pen out of my hand.

Everly tugs at him, whispering something into his ear that I can't quite make out.

"I know." He shrugs her off and walks away.

She wraps her hands around her arms as she stands next to me, watching Jamie walk around the tables and reading about each of the packages.

She glares at me and shakes her head, and then after a moment, she goes up to him and takes his arm.

This isn't going well.

It's the wrong approach.

But I have to keep trying.

She tries to pull him away, but he refuses to go.

I have successfully challenged his ego, which was my intention all along.

She tries again.

She's whispering, but I hear her mention that he doesn't have the money to bid on any of it.

I smile.

I don't either, of course.

I mean, who the hell does? Besides my father.

And I know exactly how he got all of his billions,

which doesn't exactly make me race into that line of work.

Of course, Jamie doesn't know any of this.

"You don't know anything about me," Jamie snaps at her.

His voice is loud enough for me to hear.

Everly's facing away from me, but Jamie is directly within my line of sight.

There's rage in his voice.

Tonight is not going as he had planned and that's putting everything he had worked toward in disarray.

Good, I say to myself.

I must be doing something right.

But is it enough?

Everly walks away.

Yes, yes, it is enough! Keep going and don't look back. Go! I want to yell at the top of my lungs.

She doesn't get far before he practically chases her down.

She nearly drops her drink but catches it just in time.

I'm too far away now. I can't hear a word that they're saying, but I can see the hand gestures and I can guess as to where it's headed.

She's trying to leave.

He's trying to stop her.

The more he tries to force her, the more she retreats into herself.

Their fight becomes a kind of dance where one party takes over and the other practically disappears entirely.

From across the room, I watch and hope that his anger convinces her that he's not what he seems.

He's a liar.

A sociopath.

He is a very dangerous man who is being paid a lot of money to do what he is doing.

But then just as I think that she's about to pull away completely, he changes his demeanor.

It's as if he has a realization and, suddenly, his caves his body toward hers, making himself as small as possible.

Yearning for her forgiveness, he takes her hand in his.

He is gentle and apologetic and almost kind.

Don't believe him.

Don't do it, I say to myself over and over, as if my silent pleas could somehow penetrate her soul.

More words are exchanged.

She motions for him to follow her and their fingers intertwine.

No, no, no.

Cold sweat runs down my back.

I have to stop this. I'm watching a car crash in slow motion.

She's standing on the shoulder without a worry in the world, and a driver going ninety miles an hour with the intention of hitting her is pressing the pedal to the metal.

She's about to get hit, and there's nothing I can do.

Or is there?

Instead of heading straight out of the hotel, he leads her to the bar. Another round of drinks.

Good.

This will buy me more time.

Time passes slowly when you're waiting, and it moves like molasses when you're waiting to do something but aren't sure of what exactly.

When she heads to the bathroom, I see that this is the last opportunity that I will get.

As I wait for her, I gather my thoughts and try to think of the best way to make my case. But the situation is dire and it's about to get much worse, and nothing I can possibly say can really convey that.

"You need to leave," I blurt out as soon as I see her come out.

She looks up from her phone, startled.

"What?"

I take a few steps closer to her and lower my voice. "You need to leave."

We are standing so close that I can smell her perfume, or body lotion, or whatever it is that smells like the sand and the sea and a life of innocence and love.

"You're not safe," I say, looking straight into her eyes.

She doesn't understand.

She shakes her head.

She tries to move away, but there's a wall right behind her.

"What are you talking about?" she demands.

"Something bad is going to happen."

"You're crazy," she says, walking away from me.

I take a few rushed steps to catch up to her.

"You have to believe me."

"I don't have to do anything," she says, turning to face me. "And who do you think you are, anyway?"

"I'm trying to protect you."

"From what, exactly?"

"Your date."

CHAPTER 3 - EASTON

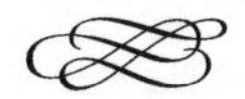

WHEN I CAN'T GET THROUGH...

My words take her by surprise.

It's as if they knock the wind out of her.

She even starts to cough, cleaning her throat over and over again, without actually making a difference.

But then, within a split moment, everything changes.

She furrows her eyebrows in disbelief and the rest of her face quickly follows.

"My date is a nice guy. That's more than what I can say about you." She looks as if I had knocked the wind out of her.

She starts to walk away.

I lost her.

Whatever I said wasn't enough.

But then she comes back.

"What the hell is your problem with Jamie, anyway? You just met him."

I hesitate, trying to find the right words.

"I can't tell you. But he's one of them."

"Who?"

"He's going to hurt you."

"You're just fucking with me," she says, shaking her head.

I grab her hand. "Don't go back in there," I whisper.

"Let me go!" She pulls away from me. "Or I'll scream."

I take a step back.

It feels a little bit like dealing with a wild animal.

She doesn't know me and doesn't trust me.

Why should she?

But my words are making an impression.

I can see it in the way her eyes are darting from place to place without staying anywhere for too long.

"Why are you doing this? Do you get some sort of high from this?"

"No, not at all," I say quietly.

She's reaching out to me for answers.

The scare tactics aren't working; all that they're doing is putting fear into her.

But she's receptive to listening.

She wants to hear me.

"I don't want to frighten you," I say softly. "I just don't know how much time you have. I can't tell you much. I just need you to run. Run home, get inside, lock the doors, and do not open them for anyone."

She shakes her head.

I'm losing her again.

"Everly, please," I plead. "Please believe me."

"But my purse is in there."

"It doesn't matter."

"No, I need it to get home. How am I going to pay for a cab?"

"I'll give you money," I say and take out my wallet.

Suddenly, he's back. He wraps his arm around her waist and pulls her close.

"You again." He glares at me and hands Everly her purse. "Let's get out of here."

Powerless to stop the car, I just stand and watch.

But when she turns her head back toward me, I try again.

"Run! Run!"

But she walks out into the hallway and disappears.

* * *

WHAT ELSE CAN I DO? I wonder, looking at the way the ice cubes bounce around the bottom of the glass. They make a loud clinking sound with each collision.

I could run after her, try to stop her from getting in the car with him.

But she doesn't know me.

The more I push, the more likely she will be to just turn to him for comfort.

No, I've made my case.

I just hope it was enough.

Besides, this isn't my business.

None of this.

I should've never come.

I hold my glass so tightly, the whites of my knuckles appear.

I know that I shouldn't be here.

I know that I don't have the power to stand up to this machine, but what happens when you are in the unique position to help someone and refuse to go that extra step?

A moment later, I'm running out of the banquet room.

I'm running down the foyer and outside.

I have to find her.

I have to stop her.

I have to do everything in my power to protect her.

PART TWO

CHAPTER 4 - EASTON

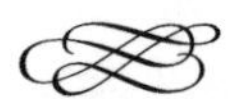

WHEN TIME GOES IN CIRCLES...

Alone in a cell for hours on end, you have a lot of time to think and reflect and relive your past.

But instead of just going back to a few individual moments like you do in everyday life, whenever a scent or an image takes you back there, now I'm living entirely in my memories.

Every day here lasts a minute and an hour and a year all at the same time.

The concept of time suddenly seems circular instead of linear.

What happened months ago now seems to have happened in another century and a moment ago.

The one thing that I am certain of is that I have loved her for a very long time.

Long before I ever met her.

It was as if everything that happened before her occurred for the sole purpose of meeting her. Is that even possible? I don't know. It's just a feeling I have and that's pretty much all I have now.

The guard comes and hands me food through a little slot in the door.

The room is cold and damp and without a single window.

In here, I don't know whether it's day or night. All I can go by is the lights which turn on at the start of the day and turn off at the end.

There is no smooth transition like there is on the outside.

No twilight, no sunrise.

One moment the beam is the fluorescent of day, and the next it's pitch black.

I don't know which I hate more.

During the day, I hate the harshness of the cold white light, which makes my eyes ache. But at night, I sometimes lie awake staring into the darkness, wishing for the warmth of soft candlelight to wrap itself around me and give me hope.

As I take a piece of the soggy bread, which is somehow both oily on one side and dry in the middle, my thoughts return to Everly.

I have loved her for years.

It was a quiet, knowing kind of love, located somewhere deep inside of me.

I haven't even met her, but it's like I always knew that she was out there and was mine to love.

Others have loved her, too.

They told her they did.

They kissed her like they did.

She said she loved them, too.

Of these things, I am certain.

But theirs was not the kind of love that I feel for her.

I remember exactly how I felt when I stood in that room looking at the spreadsheet with the names.

There were so many of them.

To my father they were potential contestants.

To me, they were potential victims.

This was the first time I'd seen their names like this, on a list.

Compiled and organized, alphabetically, by name.

I didn't know a thing about any of them, but her name jumped out at me immediately.

At the time, I thought that it was because her name was Everly.

Not the most common name out there.

But now, I think it's because I felt a familiarity with it.

It was like a part of me had known her before I ever met her.

Is that possible? I didn't think so before, but some people say that it is.

Now, I don't know.

It certainly feels like it is.

I now know that I have loved Everly even before I met her.

It's ridiculous and stupid and improbable, and I don't expect you to believe me.

Yet, it is true.

And true things do not require others to believe them for them to continue to be true.

This feeling is hard to explain, as you can imagine.

But I'll try.

I've lived with a gaping hole in my soul.

It wasn't life-threatening, and I could still function and live, but I couldn't do anything to make it go away.

To make it better.

And then Everly came along.

Breathtaking.

Quiet.

Contemplative.

Solid.

Kind.

She came into my life all of a sudden, like a breeze.

I noticed her, but I didn't notice her.

She was there, and she needed help, so I did what I could. It didn't work.

It didn't stop her from coming here.

But even when I saw her on the island all those days later, it still didn't hit me.

That she was the one I was looking for all this time.

My throat tingles and then a wave of coughing rushes through me.

My nose starts to run.

The wetness and the dampness seem to penetrate through the walls of this cell and being here for days on end has finally caught up with me.

Each cough builds somewhere in my stomach and comes out like a violent explosion. The rest of my body struggles to catch up.

It comes in waves.

One wave replaces the next one before I have the chance to catch my breath. In the end, when the assault finally starts to wane, I lie down on the thin mattress, utterly exhausted.

Think of my life as a jigsaw puzzle.

All the pieces are there.

It's complete.

Perfect, just the way it was designed.

But then, all of a sudden, another puzzle appears.

Out of nowhere.

At first, you look at it and think to yourself, I don't need another puzzle piece.

I'm done.

But the longer you hold it in the palm of your hand, the harder it is to push away.

And the thing about this puzzle piece is that it's magic.

It fits around every edge and into every nook and cranny.

Suddenly, it fills in gaps you didn't even know were there.

Suddenly, you can't imagine your puzzle being complete without it.

Everything was so perfect right before *this* happened.

I had Everly.

My father was actually going to let me marry her.

I wanted to marry her.

In a flash, I'm back there.

Hot water is running down my body.

The flow is strong, and the head is right above us, creating the illusion of a waterfall.

The light is soft and inviting, like the kind that two hundred candles would put out.

We're standing there, in the shower, holding each other.

I'm holding her.

Everly is holding me.

CHAPTER 5 - EASTON

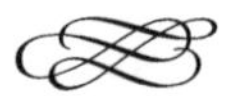

WHEN I REGRET...

I can feel her body relaxing under my hands.

It makes me feel good that I'm putting her at ease.

She trusts me.

And I trust her.

This moment is perfect.

The hotter the water gets, the more I feel myself relaxing as well.

Perhaps, this is going to be okay after all.

Maybe a life here, at least until after we are married, is the right thing to do.

I reach down for her.

I run my hands over her body.

I tell her that everything is fine.

She kisses me back in agreement.

I kneel before her and continue to run my tongue over her body.

My lips feel at home here.

I know where to go and what she likes.

She pulls my head up and kisses me back.

My hands make their way down her breasts as hers reach for my shoulders.

I like the feel of her nails digging into my skin.

Sometimes it's a bit painful, but it's a good kind of pain.

I kneel down before her again and run my hands down her stomach.

I watch as the water rushes down it and the way it moves in and out with each of her breaths.

She spreads her legs apart and I press my lips on her hipbone.

Then a knock changes everything.

The door swings open.

Guards appear.

I jump up to my feet and reach for the shower knob.

This moment should be blurry in memory, but I remember every last detail.

The large guard has the smell of cigar smoke emanating from him.

The shortest one has a buzz cut with little stray hairs on his shoulders, as if he had just had it done before the raid.

The other two are trying to keep their composure, but the look of terror in their eyes betrays them.

"What the hell are you doing?" I demand to know.

Anger is pulsating through my veins, and I'm not trying to contain it.

They don't respond.

The tallest guard opens the glass door, grabbing for me.

I push away from him, but the space is quite small and I don't want Everly to get hurt.

She tries to come in between us and the others quickly point their guns in her face.

I flip my arms with the sign of surrender.

I can't let this escalate.

They have guns and we don't.

I can't have them doing anything to hurt her.

Still, my rage gets the best of me.

"Get off me!" I yell. "Do you know who I am?"

"Easton Bay, Prince of York, you are under arrest for the murder of Christopher Weider," the guard with the buzz cut says. "You have the right to remain silent. Everything you say can and will be used against you. You have the right to an attorney—"

That's when it all goes blurry.

The guard continues to talk, but I start to yell something in return.

Why are they here?

What are they doing?

What the hell are they talking about?

Christopher Weider isn't dead!

They push me out of the bathroom.

Someone hands me a towel.

Someone else hands me my clothes and they surround me as I put them on.

Everly is out of sight now and we're in the main room. They surround me and point their guns in my face.

They aren't afraid now.

They know what they're doing.

At first, I thought they had me confused with someone else, but now I know that they know exactly who I am.

After I get dressed, the tall guard puts handcuffs on me behind my back while the one with the buzz cut continues to read me my rights.

I take a few deep breaths and stop shouting. If

whatever I say will be used against me, then I will not say another word until I speak with my lawyer.

As they take me to one holding cell and then move me to another, they treat me with kid gloves. It doesn't feel like it at the time, but in retrospect, I know that they aren't being hard on me.

Not yet.

They want me to confess.

They bring me hot tea and biscuits and when I say that I'm hungry for something more substantial, they even bring me lobster ravioli.

As I eat, the first detective comes in and tries to become my friend. He's friendly and nice, kind even.

He wants me to trust him.

I do, but that doesn't mean that I would go so far as to give him any information.

When he sees that his approach isn't working, another one comes in.

This one is old and tough and the kind that doesn't seem to have much energy for bullshit.

Not that I'm into bullshitting myself. Before completely angering him by shutting down his line of questioning, I simply listen and eat, fast.

When I take my last bite and down a few sips of tea, I finally look up to him and tell him that I have nothing to say to him and that I want to talk to a lawyer.

His anger explodes out of him, and he grabs my plate and smashes it against the wall. I'm glad that I got to finish my meal first.

Another detective comes in.

This time it's a woman.

She's tall and gorgeous and looks a bit like an actress.

She may very well be a real police officer, but I wouldn't put anything past my father.

She flirts with me. Touches my arm. Sympathizes with me.

Again, I don't fall for the bait.

They all have different approaches, but they all have the same purpose, to get me to talk.

They need my confession to seal the deal.

No, thank you.

If they want my blood, they will have to work for it, much harder than this.

My attorney finally comes to see me hours later, maybe even a whole day later. I'm not really sure.

Time back there in the holding area was even more confusing.

Looking back, I now know that it was the waiting that made it so difficult.

When you are waiting for something and you have no idea how long you will have to wait, time becomes interminable.

All I wanted was to go back to the hour before they came for me.

What would I change if I could?

Everything.

For one thing, I wouldn't be there.

As soon as we were alone, I'd take Everly and run as far away from this place as I could.

I'd take one of the boats to the neighboring island of Hamilton and then catch a flight from there. They have a few each day and they aren't as closely tracked as the flights from York. I'd also pay the pilot extra to keep quiet.

Why didn't I do this earlier?

I have asked myself this question a number of times before and I don't really have an answer.

Fear is a part of it.

But it's also something else.

Faith.

Belief.

Despite everything, I still had the trust that my father felt something for me.

Despite everything, a part of me believed that my father could never hurt me. Oh, how foolish I was.

My throat tingles again and I let out a cough.

I hope it doesn't turn into a spell and, for once, it doesn't.

I cough twice and then it's over.

I can breathe again, even though my chest feels tight.

A few days ago, I t here running a fever, covered in sweat.

At home, I would've changed the sheets and my clothes and taken a shower to make myself feel a little better.

But here, I just wrapped myself up in the threadbare blanket and waited for the shakes to go away.

In the throes of the fever, my mind focuses on only one thing, Everly.

She is my everything.

She is the only reason I keep going.

Besides my pangs of regret, which creep up into my thoughts every now and then, there are other things, too.

There are the questions of what could've happened.

How is it that Dagger is dead if I wasn't the one who killed him?

I know why they think it's me.

I'm the one with the motive.

If they think that I found out the truth about Alicia's death, then I would be their number one suspect.

But I know for certain that I didn't kill him.

So, how did he die?

And why?

CHAPTER 6 - EVERLY

WHILE I WAIT...

The walls are closing in around me.

I sit on the edge of my bed with my arms planted firmly around my knees.

Then I feel the texture of my leggings in between my fingertips.

It's soft and elastic, bouncing back with each motion as I pull it away and snap it back in place.

It's strange to say, but I feel like there's a sense of hopefulness to this elasticity.

It's the ability to take a hit and bounce back.

It's the kind of hopefulness that I thought I had only a bit ago.

I place my head on top of my knees and close my eyes.

The scene in the shower keeps running over and over again in my head.

They came for him.

They barged in.

They arrested him.

It has to be a mistake, but it sure doesn't feel like it.

You do not just barge in on the Prince of York in a compromising position with his fiancée unless you are sure that you are arresting the right person.

My thoughts run in circles over everything that happened.

Mirabelle was so sure when she said what she said.

Her words come back to me immediately.

I didn't know who Christopher Weider was until she told me that his nickname was Dagger.

"Easton killed him to avenge the death of his ex, Alicia," she said.

I broke down when I heard that, and tears started to roll down my cheeks as my thoughts went back to that moment.

Why would he do that?

He made a promise to me.

I hear Easton's voice in my head.

"There is no point in revenge," he said.

He is certain, and confident, and self-assured.

I believe him.

I trust him.

I think that he is being wise and above all this.

But what if there was another reason for him saying that?

What if he said that because Dagger was dead already?

That thought had occurred to me briefly before.

It was the flash of a realization that I had while Mirabelle had her body draped around mine for comfort.

And now that I'm alone in my room, it comes back again.

It's haunting me, trying to make me dwell on something I don't want to think about.

I want to believe that I know Easton.

I want to believe that because I love him.

But how well do we really know the ones who we are closest to?

Some people say that everyone has secrets.

Perhaps, that's true.

The only problem is that I don't really have any from him.

I was never one to keep secrets from those I

loved and it's hard for me to imagine someone doing that to me.

But what do I really know about Easton?

We haven't had enough time together in the real world to really get to know each other as people.

There's yet another alternative, of course.

He may not be a liar in general.

He may be the person that I got to know and love.

And he may have this one secret.

Perhaps he did kill Dagger to avenge his first love, and, perhaps, he didn't tell me about it to protect me.

What good was it for me to know something like that?

I take a deep breath.

My tears have dried.

My thoughts are becoming more clear.

I still don't know the truth, but I am eager to find out.

I want to be angry with him for doing this to me, to us, for dashing my hopes of being happy - as happy as someone could be in York.

But I can't.

The one thing that I do know about Easton is he isn't a hothead.

Whatever he did or didn't do, he did with thought and deliberateness. And that's what scares me.

A knock at the door breaks me out of my trance.

"Come in!"

The door opens and Mirabelle comes in with a tray of food and a small teapot. She places it on the bed and sits down next to me.

"Are you okay?"

She puts her hand on top of mine.

I shrug and reach for a piece of toast.

It feels unfamiliar and almost tangy on my tongue.

I haven't had anything to eat in hours.

"It's going to be okay, right?" I ask, looking up at her for comfort.

Somehow, over the last few weeks, Mirabelle has become something of a mother figure to me.

She works for the King, but she has always shown me kindness and has given me sound advice and I really appreciate that.

Besides some friends I have made here, who have become eliminated, she is probably the one who I am closest to of everyone.

"It's going to be okay, right?" I ask again, looking for some level of hope.

She doesn't make eye contact with me.

Instead, she just squeezes my hand and looks away.

She is getting on in years, but it is only around her eyes where her real age is somewhat visible.

Looking at her now, she seemed to have aged overnight.

"What's wrong?" I demand to know.

My whole body is starting to shake and I can't make it stop.

I shake her hand, but she still doesn't respond.

"Tell me!"

Mirabelle takes a deep breath.

"There's going to be a trial," she finally says. "I'm sorry."

I hear the words that she is saying, but I don't understand.

"What do you mean? What kind of trial?"

"They are going to have a trial to determine if he is guilty or not guilty of killing Dagger."

"And is that...bad?" I ask.

"It's not good," she says, shaking her head. "The jurors aren't going to be exactly non-biased. His father is going to pick the presiding judge."

"But his father...the King...he surely doesn't want his son, of all people, to be found guilty of killing someone. Right? I mean, Easton is the Prince of York."

"He is, yes. But Dagger was one of the King's closest confidants. They go way back."

"But Easton is his son," I whisper. "He won't let his son be convicted."

Mirabelle shrugs, and in that shrug I see that she is on the verge of giving up hope.

"I'm sorry, Everly," she says, taking my hand in hers.

CHAPTER 7 - EVERLY

WHILE WE WAIT...

Mirabelle stays with me even though she doesn't have to.

She wraps her arms around me and finally tells me that it's all going to be okay.

Of course, now it's too late.

I needed to hear that right in the beginning, then maybe I would've believed her.

But now?

What's there to say now?

"So, what do I do now?" I ask, pouring myself a cup of tea.

I bite into a biscuit and look at her.

The lines around her face straighten out, relaxing the tension.

"You are not a suspect, of course."

I nod as if I understand, but in reality, this means very little to me.

"You are a part of the court for now. So, you will get the chance to socialize and live here until...the trial."

"And then?"

Mirabelle looks away.

I take another bite of my biscuit and wait.

She's refusing to meet my eyes.

Wait, a second. What's going on here?

"You are a very desirable woman," she says after a few moments.

"What do you mean?"

"I mean, that men want you."

"That has hardly ever been the case," I say, waving my hand in her direction.

"Well, you are here."

"What are you getting at?"

"I've heard some rumors," Mirabelle finally says. "Abbott has his eye on you."

I shake my head.

"What do you mean?" I ask with my mouth full of food.

"People are saying that if Easton is found guilty, then you will likely have to marry Abbott."

Abbott?

No, no, no.

Abbott is horrible.

He's menacing and dangerous and not in any of those good ways.

He is the devil incarnate.

He is capable of the darkest acts.

"It's just a rumor, but that's what I heard. Please, let's just take this one day at a time."

My whole body starts to shake.

I can't deal with this again.

Suddenly, everything that happened to me in the dungeons comes flooding back.

Every stare.

Every move.

Every stranger.

They come in flashes and I cower into myself.

I wrap my arms around my knees and bury my head in between.

"It's going to be okay, Everly," Mirabelle says over and over again.

She's right next to me, but I can barely hear her.

A loud alert goes off on her phone. She looks down at the screen and says that she has to go.

I don't stop rocking my body as I watch her leave the room.

When the door closes behind her, it makes a

loud clinking sound, which somehow pushes me out of my trance.

No, I say to myself. No, hell, no.

There's no way in hell I'm marrying that sadist. But what can I do?

I find myself pacing the room, trying to think of the possibilities.

For one, I have to get out of this room.

I have to stop acting as if I were guilty of something, and I have to stop bringing suspicion onto Easton.

No, I will go downstairs and hold my head up high.

He did nothing wrong because I know that he didn't.

I don't know if I will be able to convince the king of this matter, but at least I will convince the others.

The last thing I want to do is to go downstairs and talk to anyone about anything.

But I have to.

I need to pretend that everything is fine.

And I need to start making my own connections in this place.

Mirabelle tells me a lot, but I can't just rely on her.

All walls have ears, especially those with many rooms and many servants.

People talk, and I need to hear them talking.

I need friends.

I can't be a recluse if I want to survive.

Information is power.

Knowledge is power.

I desperately need both.

I take a deep breath and head straight to the bathroom.

There I run a brush through my hair, toss on some dry shampoo so it actually looks moderately clean, and start putting on my face.

Makeup has the ability to transform my mood and that's exactly what I need.

I need to feel beautiful because it's the only way I'm going to exude that for others to feel as well.

Foundation goes on first, followed by eyebrow tint, eyeliner, and mascara.

I don't know how to do false lashes, but I really wish I did.

This time I even opt for lipstick and a bit of blush.

I look at myself in the mirror.

I look pretty.

Confident.

If you look closely, you can probably see the remnants of tears, but only if you know what you're looking for.

I head to the closet and change into a different pair of yoga pants, the ones with the crisscross pattern at the bottom, as well as a clean tank top.

I pull on a new long sleeve blouse, which hangs open at the bottom, to keep myself warm in the air-conditioned air.

The clothes aren't dramatically different, but they are new and clean and a sign that I'm not moping around in bed.

I give myself one more glance over in the mirror.

The outfit is casual, but well put together and my makeup is my warpaint.

"You're ready," I say to myself. "Now, go kick some ass."

CHAPTER 8 - EVERLY

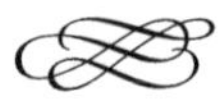

WHILE WE COMPARE STORIES...

Of course, the idea of kicking ass and actually kicking ass are quite different creatures.

I don't have a plan.

My goal is to just go mingle and make friends and talk to people I haven't talked to yet.

As an introvert who has a high level of anxiety when it comes to talking to people, this is quite a difficult task, but it's enough for now.

I am in the information gathering stage.

I need to know things that I can't possibly know unless I talk to them.

The first person I encounter is one of the older female servants dressed in a gray jumpsuit with her hair up in a bun.

I saw her before serving us dinner and collecting plates.

I don't know her name and she avoids eye contact with me.

When I slow down to say something to her, she speeds up her walking pace and rushes past me.

A moment later, she's at the other side of the hallway.

That went well, I say to myself.

Luckily, in the large-open-floorplan kitchen, dining room, living room area I find my girls. Olivia is lying on the couch watching television.

Savannah is making a shake and writing down food in her food journal and Teal is curled up with a book in a recliner.

When I come in, Catalina comes from behind me and throws her arms around me.

"Hey!" she whispers into my ear. "How are you?"

She has short-length hair with shine and volume that would make any hair model jealous.

It never seems to fall flat or get oily or dull.

Very much unlike my own hair.

Her embrace is warm and comforting.

She is probably the one I know the least out of the group, but it's nice to know that she is cheering me on.

"As good as can be expected," I say after she pulls away from me.

She tucks a few strands of hair behind my ear and gives me a squeeze on my fingers.

"We were so worried," Teal says, wrapping her arms around me as well. "I mean, we couldn't believe that they arrested him like that. And when we saw Mirabelle walk in, you...you looked so—"

She lets her words go without finishing the sentence.

She doesn't need to.

I don't remember seeing them at all, but I do know how I felt in that moment.

"Let's...um...talk about something else for a second," I say. "Would that be okay?"

"Yes, yes, of course," they all say in unison.

As I head toward the fridge, Olivia intercepts me and asks me what she can make.

I don't really know off the top of my head.

I don't even know what's inside.

I open it and stare at the contents.

Somehow, this is even less helpful.

"How about some scrambled eggs with toast and berries? We have some great blueberries and raspberries here," Olivia suggests.

I nod with a shrug.

That sounds as good as anything else.

As she cooks, the girls make an effort to stay off the topic of Easton.

But it's hard.

This place unites us.

It's also not clear where the topic of Easton begins and ends.

Can they talk about York?

Can they talk about how they got here?

And what about their lives now?

They were all going to be eliminated and then they weren't.

The king had announced that they will all be my ladies in waiting, but what about now?

To avoid all of these topics, they focus on the weather instead.

After a long discussion of the pros and cons of humidity for the hair and the skin, they shift their forced conversation to the topic of rain.

"It has been raining quite a lot here, right?" Savannah asks. "Is it always like this?"

"It usually rains a lot in Florida in the summers," Teal says.

"But how far away are we from Florida?" Catalina asks.

No one responds.

It's as if they all stop in their tracks and stare at her.

I glance at Catalina.

She freezes in place with the expression of regret.

She brought the conversation back around to reality, the very thing that we have been trying to avoid.

"Okay, I'm sorry," I say, breaking the silence. "Let's not do this."

They wait for me to elaborate.

"Let's not lie to each other anymore. This place is this den of lies and I can't stand it anymore."

They nod, hanging their heads. Olivia hands me my plate.

"I'll start," I say, digging into the eggs.

I start in the beginning, where it all began.

I tell them about how I met Jamie and how he seemed too good to be true.

Well, little did I know that he was.

I tell them about the charity event.

Then I tell them about the spiked drink.

I tell them about waking up in the dungeons. I don't sugar coat a thing and I tell them everything.

Well, almost everything.

I don't mention Easton.

I don't mention his warnings or his attempts at trying to protect me.

I don't know why exactly, except that I'm not ready to share that.

The girls nod in unison until I get to the dungeon part.

Then they look surprised.

"You weren't down there?" I ask.

They shake their heads.

I guess something about what they said here was true.

"Did you get a gold box invitation?" Teal asks.

I take a deep breath.

It's the moment of truth.

I decide not to hold anything back.

"No," I say, shaking my head. "I just said that because you all said you did so I didn't want to...raise any suspicions."

"I didn't get one either," Teal admits. "Did you?"

Catalina and Olivia and Savannah all nod.

They tell their stories.

The broad strokes are all basically a match to mine.

Mysterious man asks them on a date.

He looks like a keeper, but he refuses to take things further, sexually.

It's an unlikely choice in the contemporary dating world, but they find it endearing just like I did.

Perhaps, they found a man with a tinge -old-fashioned values to him, they think. Little do they know that he was forbidden from having any sexual contact with them.

That part is so much less romantic.

"Why do you think only some of us got gold boxes?" Catalina asks.

I don't have a good answer.

Neither does anyone else.

But we speculate.

After coming up with a few possibilities, Savannah suggests that maybe it was just a test.

"What do you mean?" I ask.

"Well, this place is all about tests, right? They're out there analyzing our every move. So, maybe they just threw that in to see if you would both just lie and conform with what all the rest of us said or if you would tell the truth?"

"I went along with you, so what does that say about me?" I ask.

"I have no idea," Savannah says.

We all shrug and stare at each other.

"One thing is for sure," Olivia says. "This place is a complete mind-fuck."

CHAPTER 9 - EVERLY

WHILE I MAKE FRIENDS...

There's something about sharing stories that creates a connection between people.

As we sit here around the kitchen island, we talk and realize that we are not that different after all.

I thought that we had similarities before, but it wasn't until this very moment that I realize that it is our trauma that really binds us to each other.

When I first got to York, I thought that everyone but me wanted to be here.

I thought it was their dream come true, but how wrong I was.

They all thought the same as well and so we all kept silent. We all kept our secrets to ourselves.

It was probably the right thing to do at the time, but it feels good to come clean now.

There is still one thing that I want to ask them, and I hope that they tell me the truth. I take a deep breath before diving in.

“What about Abbott?”

“What about him?” Teal asks.

I take another breath and then tell them what happened when I got into my room.

They listen silently without a single response.

When I’m finished, Savannah starts to cry.

Teal wraps her arms around her and Catalina presses up against her as well.

“He did the same thing to me,” Savannah confesses.

“Me, too,” the other two add. We all hang our heads as we take a moment to commiserate.

The details of what happened to each of us vary, but the broad strokes are the same. The only difference being that the others didn’t fight him off.

Their faces are scrunched up with regret.

“I just got so scared,” Savannah says.

“Me, too. I just froze,” Catalina says.

Teal nods along.

“It was probably a good thing,” I say and tell them what happened to me.

They listen, and this time reach out to comfort me.

We hold each other for a few moments until I pull away.

There is so much left unsaid in this conversation and yet these details aren't that important to fill in.

We all know that Abbott is the devil incarnate and we don't need to relive everyone's experience to confirm this.

"I have to tell you something," Teal says after a moment. "I heard some of the staff talking about Easton and you and what is going to happen."

I nod and wait for her to continue

"They were saying that if Easton is convicted, then you might have to marry Abbott."

Her eyes search mine for a sign that I understand, but my face remains expressionless. I stare into space.

I came here to make friends and to hear rumors, but this is not the knowledge that I want to hear.

I want to hear something else. I want them to tell me that nothing bad is going to happen. I want them to tell me that Mirabelle is wrong.

"Everly?" Olivia asks. "Are you okay?"

I take a deep breath. "I don't know," I say after a moment. "That's what Mirabelle told me, too."

"You have to think positively," Olivia says. "Easton didn't kill anyone, and he's not going to get convicted."

"Yes, you're right," I say.

Unfortunately, the tone of my voice is hardly convincing.

"He didn't do it, right?" Teal asks.

I look at her with a blank stare.

"Right?" Savannah asks.

"No, he didn't," I say definitively. "He didn't do anything wrong."

They may be my new friends, but I am not foolish enough to share how I really feel about this.

In truth, I am not sure.

I'm not sure of anything anymore.

What if Easton did do it?

What if he did it before he ever asked me to marry him?

He told me he didn't.

He told me that we had nothing to worry about, but now I have doubts.

Now, I'm questioning everything.

"Why do they think he did it?" Olivia asks.

I don't know if they know about Alicia and I'm not sure if I should tell them.

Despite my best efforts to open up, I find it

difficult to open up completely. I've shared my story, but Alicia's story is not mine to share.

This place is still dark and dangerous, and I need every speck of ammunition I can get.

"I don't know." I shrug and shake my head. "I have no idea why they would arrest him."

Fearing that this is not enough information, I decide to give them something else and delve into the details of his arrest.

As I lay it all out there, all the details of our shower scene and everything that went down, I watch their reaction.

They hang on every word.

"I can't believe they barged in on you...like that," Savannah finally says after I finish.

"I had no idea what was going on," I say. "That's why I was a little out of it afterward."

"Yes, of course," she agrees, again putting her hand around my shoulder. "And then, when Mirabelle came to my room and told me what might happen if he is found guilty, I just couldn't deal with being alone anymore."

Catalina, Teal, and Olivia come over and drape themselves around me as well.

It feels false to say this to some degree, but deep down what I'm saying is true.

I've come to think of these women as my friends and I want their support and love.

I need it actually.

To make it out of here alive, I will need a lot more than that.

As they continue to talk among themselves, my thoughts quickly return to Easton.

How is he?

How is he feeling?

Are they hurting him?

What is he doing right now?

Will I ever see him again?

Will we ever be together again?

And, of course, did he do it?

PART THREE

CHAPTER 10 - EASTON

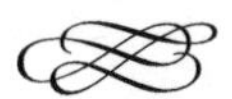

WHEN THE ATTORNEY COMES IN...

In the morning, with my breakfast, the guard tells me that my attorney is going to come to see me in the afternoon and suddenly the day starts to drag on.

Over the last few days, I've gotten used to just sitting here and letting my thoughts wander around in circles, and now, suddenly, I have something to look forward to.

Having never come in contact with the justice system here at York, or anywhere else for that matter, I didn't know who I was supposed to contact when I asked for an attorney.

So, the officers gave me a list of names and I called the number right in the middle.

The guy who showed up wasn't much to look at and seemed to be afraid of his own shadow.

He stayed with me when they questioned me, saying very little on my behalf. HIs only piece of advice was to keep my mouth shut, which I already knew.

Not knowing who else to contact, I requested another person from the list. Third name down.

John Madden Thompson.

And that's who is going to come see me today.

When the guards come to get me, they put shackles around my legs and handcuffs around my hands.

No one speaks as we walk down the long hallway, illuminated by hard white light, and the only sound that echoes around is the sound of metal I make with each step.

I'm supposed to feel thankful for the fact that they put the handcuffs on my hands in the front rather than the back, but I don't.

They lead me through a set of double doors, which each have to be opened one at a time, and then into a large conference room.

The lighting is pleasant here, with natural light streaming in through the large windows. They place me near one, and I watch as the palm tree outside sways in the wind.

I close my eyes and imagine the feel of the breeze on my face and the taste of the salt in the air.

I run my fingers over the table and linger on the natural grain of the wood.

All the ones in my cell are made of hard plastic, and I have almost forgotten how nice it feels to touch something natural, something which was once alive.

Unfortunately, I don't have much time to myself in this place.

Just as I stare at the sunlight wrapping itself around the long, tattered leaves of the palm tree, the door at the far end of the room opens and a guard walks in, followed by a large imposing man with pepper gray hair.

He is dressed in a heavy suit, which belongs more in the cold Connecticut winter than it does on this Caribbean island in the middle of the summer.

When the man gets closer, I see the beads of sweat that are rolling off his large forehead and the redness of his cheeks.

"Easton?" he asks, trying to catch his breath.

I nod.

He extends his hand, and when I don't reach out

mine fast enough, he grabs for it, practically forcing his handshake on me.

"You can call me Tiger," he says, putting down his briefcase and loosening his tie.

"Tiger?"

"My real name is John Madden Thompson, but everyone calls me Tiger," he explains without really offering much of an explanation.

Tiger seems to be kind of an inappropriate name for someone in their mid-fifties, but what the hell do I know?

It takes Tiger a few moments to get organized.

He opens his briefcase, takes out some files, gets out a pen, and pulls out a yellow legal pad.

Then he turns his attention to me.

"Tell me everything," he says.

I stare at him and shake my head a little.

"I'm not sure where you want me to start."

"In the beginning."

"What do you know already?"

"Let's say I know nothing."

I narrow my eyes.

"Easton, I may know some things, but that should be none of your concern. I am here to listen to your version."

"You mean the truth, right?"

"Yes, of course," he says, but I don't believe him.

"What about...?" I let my words trail off and point to the recording equipment all around us.

"It's turned off."

I don't know if I believe him, but what choice do I have.

I can say nothing and this meeting won't go anywhere.

"How do you know?"

"I watched them turn it off."

"They could've turned it back on again," I insist.

Tiger opens his briefcase and turns it to face me. Inside, I see small recording microphones and wires.

"You are the only prisoner in this area," he says. "I made sure they took it all down."

Satisfied, I give him a nod.

"I am not an idiot, Easton. I am here to help."

I shake my head again and inhale deeply.

"They think I killed Dagger," I say after a moment. "But I didn't. I really wanted to, especially after I found out that my father had ordered him to kill Alicia, but I didn't."

"Why not?"

I shrug. "Honestly, I was biding my time. Plus, I wanted to keep Everly safe."

The longer I talk, the more I open up to him.

I don't have many cards to play, so if he turns on me, then so what?

I'm pretty much already a doomed man.

But something tells me that he's not going to.

Tiger listens and nods his head and takes copious notes.

At first, I find it unnerving to have someone write down almost every word you say, but after a bit, I hardly notice it at all.

Instead, I just open my mouth and talk.

I tell him about Alicia, and I tell him about our plans.

"What were you going to do after you left?" Tiger interrupts me. "Were you planning on reporting on what's going on here?"

CHAPTER 11 - EASTON

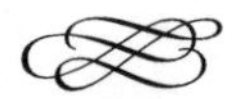

WHILE HE PRESSES ME...

I stare at him. What does he know exactly?

"I know, Easton. I know about the competitions. I know how the king picks his wives every other year."

"You do?" I whisper.

He nods and asks me about our plans again. All doubts about whether or not this place is bugged vanish from my mind.

He would never ask anything like that or admit anything like that to me if he still had an inkling that our conversation was being listened to.

"Well?" Tiger prods me.

I look away from him, unable to meet his gaze.

"No," I say after a moment.

My cheeks flush with shame.

"I want to say yes that we had plans about exposing this place, but we didn't. We were young. We just wanted to get away. Back then, I still had something of a warm feeling toward my father and brother. After my mother's death, they were the only family I had left. I didn't want to make things hard. I just wanted to...get away."

"I can see that this is painful for you to talk about," Tiger says. "I'm sorry about that."

I shrug and look away.

"It is, but it's also good to get it out. I loved Alicia, but I also saw her as a way out of here. She gave me the courage to step away from this place, and I'm just so sorry that she had to pay the ultimate price for that."

I bury my head in my hands.

He puts his arm around me and I don't push it away.

I haven't had genuine human contact for a long time and it feels good to create a connection, however tenuous.

"I'm sorry," I say after a moment, lifting my head. "I didn't mean to get so...emotional."

Tiger gives me a moment and then jumps into the next line of questioning.

How did I find out about the King's order to kill Alicia?

Does anyone know that I did?

What did I intend to do about it?

How did I feel about it?

I answer all of his questions to the best of my ability and he continues to make notes without much commentary.

As we talk, one hour turns into two and then into three.

But instead of feeling tired and drained, I feel invigorated.

I had forgotten how nice it is to talk to someone who is willing to listen.

"Thank you for being so forthcoming, Easton," Tiger says, flipping the pages of his yellow legal pad to the front.

He had managed to fill up close to half the pages with his scribbles.

I hope that they are useful.

"I hope you don't lose that thing," I say. "It's got a lot of useful info to put me away for good."

"In terms of motive, yes," Tiger says. "But it's also a good record to exonerate you."

"That's if you believe everything in there, which I doubt they will."

Tiger gives me a little nod.

"You believe me, right?" I ask. His eyes meet mine.

"Yes, of course."

"You don't sound...convinced."

"I don't have to believe you to represent you."

Somewhere in the pit of my stomach, anger starts to tingle and rise.

"I know lawyers like to say that. At least, I've seen lawyers say that a lot in movies, but that's not what I want you to say. No," I correct myself. "That's not what I want you to believe."

He shrugs.

"What is it that you don't believe?" I demand to know.

"Why is it so important to you that I do?" he asks instead.

"Because I'm fucking innocent. I'm an innocent man sitting here in a cell, awaiting trial, so that the jury, or the judge, or whoever is going to do it is going to find me guilty of doing something I should've fucking done!"

My anger springs me out of my chair and onto my feet.

"Do you know how that *fucking* feels, man?" I demand. "It feels like shit. I should've killed that son of a bitch. I should've put a bullet right through his skull. Or better yet, I should've locked him inside a boat taking on water, so he could suffocate or drown or both. So he could spend the last few moments of his life trying to do something to break free all to no avail. But I didn't."

"Why?" Tiger asks calmly, even though I'm standing a few inches away from his face ready to punch him.

"Because I was in love. I loved Alicia, at least I thought I did, but then I met Everly. I don't want to compare. It's not fair to Alicia, but when I met Everly...it was, game over, you know? This is the woman for me. This is the woman I will love forever no matter what. No matter if she breaks my heart and stomps on it and then throws it into the garbage. I will love her forever because you can't help who you love. And that's why I didn't avenge Alicia's death. Because I thought I had another chance to start my life over. I thought that my father would let me marry her and we could start our lives together. And I took a chance. I believed him. What a fucking idiot I was."

The words topple over each other and come out all at once, like a geyser or a waterfall, strong and powerful and unstoppable.

"So, the thing is that," I say after I gather my thoughts a bit, "if you don't believe me, then I don't really need your representation. I'm done believing in my father and in York. I can represent myself just as well. I just don't want someone up there who doesn't believe me. I can be convicted of this crime just as easily without you."

When I finish talking, the anger that's been boiling up within me suddenly simmers down.

I've said my piece and that's enough.

Without another word, I turn around and walk away from him.

There are guards on the other side of the door, but they are turned away from me.

"Easton." Tiger gets up and catches up with me right before I reach the door to get the guard's attention.

I don't stop, but then he puts his hand on my shoulder.

"Easton, I'm sorry," he says. "I believe you."

I turn around.

Face-to-face with him, I read his face.

Is he telling me the truth or is he just telling me what I want to hear?

"I didn't mean to cause offense."

I shrug and take a step back.

I need the space to judge him more accurately.

He doesn't say anything for a moment, so I wait.

I've said enough and now it's his turn to make his case.

"Easton, lawyers are typically not concerned with whether their clients are guilty or not guilty," Tiger says.

I cross my hands across my chest. This is not what I want, or need, to hear, but I continue to listen.

"Whether a client is guilty or not guilty has no effect on our ability to do our jobs," he continues. "But I want to make one thing absolutely clear to you."

He takes a step forward and looks straight into my eyes.

"I believe you and I will do everything in my power to help you."

CHAPTER 12 - EASTON

WHILE SOMEONE SURPRISES ME…

Tiger leaves a few minutes later and they tell me to wait. I'm not complaining.

Here, I can look out of the window at the puffy clouds hanging low against the blue sky. I watch as the long leaves of the palm tree reach for the heavens above.

It sways in the breeze and is free in all the ways that I am not.

I expect them to come for me in a few minutes, but when a guard does appear, he just tells me to wait.

"You have another visitor coming soon."

He doesn't elaborate and leaves soon after.

But he does have a little smile on his face and that curl of the lips makes me wonder.

My heart can't help but skip a beat.

Another visitor?

What if? Can it be *her*?

I imagine Everly walking through the door.

What a sight for weary eyes.

Her hair will bounce with each step and her eyes will twinkle when they meet mine. She will wrap her arms around me and I will know that everything is okay, even if it's just okay for this moment.

She will ask me about how I've been, but I will interrupt her and insist on hearing about her first.

How is she?

How have they been treating her?

Has Abbott threatened her again?

Is she safe?

These are all the questions that have run through my mind in loops ever since I've been trapped here, in purgatory.

The guards haven't said a word and Tiger didn't know a thing.

And now...finally...I will have my answer.

My hands get sweaty with anticipation.

I'm going to see her so soon.

I try to focus my attention on the window outside, but I keep glancing back at the door. Any minute now, I'm going to see her.

I'm going to run my fingers through her hair and pull her close to me.

I'm going to inhale her beautiful scent and press my lips onto hers.

And there, in her mouth, with her body wrapped around mind, I will be home again.

The door swings open.

And *he* walks through it.

My head starts to buzz.

My vision gets blurry.

I blink and he's a few feet closer to me.

I blink again and he's right in front of me.

Cocky.

Entitled.

With his shoulders back and with that arrogant smile on his face.

"What are you doing here?" I ask.

He shrugs, staring me down.

"What the *fuck* are you doing here, Abbott?" I say, raising my voice.

"I'm here, just to say hello. I miss you, brother."

"I doubt that."

It takes me a moment to recover from the shock of seeing him instead of Everly, but I do my best to not let that show.

To show any sort of vulnerability around Abbott is a big mistake.

He will pounce on it immediately and I will live to regret it.

"So, so, so," he says, taking a few steps away from me and then back toward me.

He's pacing, biding his time.

He is making me wait.

Then something occurs to me.

I don't have to be here.

I don't have to listen to whatever lies he's about to spew at me.

Without another word, I walk past him and toward the door.

"Where are you going?" he yells after me.

I don't bother to answer him.

Instead, I wave for the guard and wait for him to open it.

"I want to go back to my cell," I tell him.

"The Prince of York has requested to speak with you," the guard says. "You will talk to him for as long as he wants."

His words take me aback, but he just turns around and closes the door in front of me.

"I'm the *fucking* Prince of York!" I pound on the window. "Doesn't that fucking matter?"

The guard just turns his back to me.

"Fuck!"

"You see, my dear brother, you may be the Prince of York, but our ranks aren't exactly the same anymore."

"What happened to being innocent until proven guilty?" I ask, turning to face him.

"Eh, you know, this is York. Things are a little different here."

I shake my head.

"What the *fuck* do you want?" I ask.

"Well, I just wanted to come here and see how you are," he mocks me. "How are you holding up? Father is so worried."

"I'm sure," I say, my voice dripping in sarcasm.

"You have to understand it from his position. Dagger was one of his closest friends. They go way back. And when he found out that you
killed him—"

"I didn't kill him."

"Of course not. I know that, but that's not what he thinks."

How does he know that? Where is he going with this?

"Why does he think that?" I ask.

Abbott shrugs. "I don't know exactly, but I have

my suspicions. I mean, he did have Alicia killed, right?"

I shake my head. How does he know all of this?

"See, the thing is, brother, that I have a lot of eyes and ears in this place. I know what Dagger did on Father's request. I knew that even before you found out about it."

Blood seems to drain away from my body and pools somewhere in my toes. I feel my face turning a light shade of green as I let his words settle into my mind.

"C'mon now, don't look so shocked," Abbott continues.

"What do you want?" I ask. "Why are you here?"

"I just wanted to talk with you. Maybe make a deal of some sort."

"Deal?"

"Yeah, I wanted to see if you were possibly open to making some sort of deal."

I narrow my eyes.

Abbott is smart.

He's a sadist, but he's cunning.

He is not reaching out to me because he wants to help me.

I have something he wants.

But what?

CHAPTER 13 - EASTON

WHILE HE ASKS ME FOR SOMETHING...

Abbott takes a moment to gather his thoughts.

He must really want this.

I know him, at least as much as I possibly can know him.

Abbott has been a dark part of my family for a very long time, but to say that I know him would be a grave misunderstanding.

I don't know him, just like he doesn't know me. But I do know how to read him.

"What do you want, Abbott?" I ask with my patience growing thin. "I'm tired of games."

"I know, me, too."

I scoff at this, but keep my mouth shut.

Abbott is nothing but games.

He likes them because he likes to win.

But the only reason he ever wins is because he almost always has an advantage.

"I want to help you," Abbott says.

His face softens a bit.

There's an actual look of concern on it.

"This...this whole thing..." he says, pointing his finger around the space. "This isn't good. Father has never done anything like this before."

I shrug.

He's right.

I know he's right, but what can I do about it?

"I mean, he sent me away. He sent you away. To teach us a lesson. But a public trial like this? He really thinks you killed him, Easton. And he's out for blood."

I stare straight ahead.

At him, but through him at the same time.

My eyes feel like they are almost glazing over.

"Easton, I'm here to help you. Don't you get that?" Abbott shakes me out of my stupor.

Everything in my body is screaming not to believe him, but that one aching feeling in the back of my mind is bringing out doubts.

What if he's *not* lying?

What if he's actually here for me?

"I'm sorry I was such a dick. I'm sorry about everything, okay?" Abbott says. "But I'm just worried about you. Father is pissed, and he wants revenge. He can't believe what you've done."

Suddenly, my eyes jump into focus.

"What I've done? I haven't done anything!"

"You didn't?"

"No, of course not. This whole thing is a…sham." I scramble around for the right word, but nothing comes to mind.

"Don't you believe me?" I ask.

I didn't know this before, but there's something inside of an innocent man accused of a crime he didn't commit that screams out to anyone who will listen.

Abbott has been my brother and my enemy for approximately equal amounts of time in my life, and yet even with him, I feel the need to prove myself.

Someone has to believe me. They just have to!

"I thought that you did," Abbott says slowly.

"I didn't," I say quietly. "So, what kind of deal did you want to make?"

Without missing a beat, he says, "I want you to plead guilty."

It takes me a moment to process this request.

"What? Hell no!" I add quickly.

"Hear me out, okay? I want you to plead guilty to butter Father up. He has been having some issues with Dagger and I don't think he's as hung up on his death as he wants everyone to think."

I shake my head.

Abbott takes a step closer to me and puts his arm around my shoulder.

"If you agree to plead guilty, then I will go to Father and try to convince him to give you leniency. I will ask him to go easy on you."

"And why would he do that?"

"Because you're his son after all. But you know how he is. He will never back down. He will never admit a mistake. So, if you go ahead with this trial, then you'll go away for a very long time."

"I'm probably going to go away for a very long time either way," I say. "I want to at least fight for my freedom."

"It's not black and white like this, Easton. Life is about shades of gray. You say you didn't do it, but if you plead guilty, then you'll probably get two years at Hamilton. It's bad, but it's not life there. And I'm pretty sure they'll give you life if you are found guilty at trial."

I look away from him and clench my jaw.

He's right.

I hate to admit it, but he is.

At least, when it comes to assessing Father's state of mind and his ability to hold on to grudges.

"Life at Hamilton? I'd probably rather be executed," I mumble.

"Yeah, I was there for a few days. It's not pretty," Abbott adds. "But they won't give you the death penalty."

"And why not?"

"Because you're a fucking royal. And not just a royal. A prince. No, they'll make you suffer to the end of your days, but they won't get rid of you. Your fate will be even worse. Everyone will just forget about you."

The thought of that sends shivers through my body.

Not just because I'm a human being who doesn't want to be forgotten, but also because of the fate that represents.

Life goes on on the outside, and I will be in a cell somewhere rotting away for good, completely forgotten to the world.

No one will know that I'm there and the more time that will pass, the less likely that anyone will remember ever again.

"Make this deal, brother," Abbott whispers into

my ear. “Make this deal and I will do everything in my power to help you.”

I look into his eyes. I still don’t trust him, but I don’t know if this an option I have anymore.

He’s asking me to gamble with my life on a promise.

A promise with the man who betrayed me in numerous ways over the years.

Can I do that?

Of course, I can.

But is it wise?

Probably not. Yet, what option do I have?

“Why are you doing this?” I ask him. “What’s in it for you?”

“Nothing. I just want to help my brother.”

I stare at him. I try to read what I can from his expression, but it gives me nothing. And then, suddenly, there’s a little curl of the lips upward.

“No,” I say definitively.

CHAPTER 14 - EASTON

WHILE I SEE RED…

Abbott stares at me in disbelief and takes a step backward, surprised.

There are certain moments in which you just have to go with your gut.

There is no proof and you don't really require any.

We are quick to dismiss these moments, but they can change everything.

And what are they? It's usually something small.

Insignificant.

Difficult to pinpoint.

Something gives you a bad feeling and you should just go with it.

Sometimes, it's a shiver running up the back of your spine.

Sometimes, it's an ache in the pit of your stomach.

Sometimes, it's a sharp prickly pain that rushes through you at the sight of something else. In my case, it was the last thing.

As soon as I saw that curl of the lips, that beginning of a little smile, I knew that something was wrong.

It's not that much of a leap for me to not believe what my brother says, but still, until I saw his little conniving smile, I was giving him the benefit of the doubt.

"No, thank you," I say.

"You don't believe me?" Abbott asks.

The expression on his face changes from begging to a little harsh, but I don't see any anger in his eyes.

Yet.

Is it coming? I wonder.

"I don't know. It's not really about you. I just...it's not something I can do right now."

"Why not?"

"I didn't kill Dagger and I can't say that I did."

"Even to get a lighter sentence? Are you a fucking idiot?"

"I don't have any guarantees of what would happen if I do take the deal. So...I just can't. I mean,

I'm not sure I would anyway. That's a big thing to confess, you know."

Abbott starts to walk in circles, shaking his head.

"Why do you care so much?" I ask.

"Because I want...what's best for you. You're my fucking brother."

I try to explain again, but he doesn't want to listen.

Suddenly, I'm starting to have doubts.

Am I really assessing this situation correctly?

What if he is telling the truth?

I try to imagine my decision if anyone else would've presented me with the deal. For instance, what if it were Everly?

Everly would never ask me to confess to something I didn't do.

I know that for sure.

But two years in prison versus a lifetime is something that's difficult to dismiss.

Still, a promise like that is not something she or anyone else could keep unless it's the king himself.

And so far, I have not heard that kind of proposition from my father.

"You know, you are such an idiot, Easton," Abbott says, interrupting my train of thought.

I look at him.

I know that he's not happy with my decision and when he's not happy, he will make sure that no one is happy.

"Here I am offering you the deal of a lifetime, and what are you doing? Turning it down? Well, fuck that. And fuck you!" Abbott says.

I'm taken aback a bit by his reaction.

"Why do you care so much? You barely cared before. And don't tell me it's because you're my brother."

"Why not? It's the truth."

"I sort of doubt that."

He opens his mouth as if he's about to say something else, but then he closes it and starts to laugh.

The small, quiet chuckle quickly morphs into a loud thunderous laugh.

"What's so funny?"

"Hold on a second," he says, holding out his index finger.

Waves of laughter move his body from side to side as I look at him with confusion.

"Fine, fine. I'll come clean," he says after a moment, finally getting a hold of himself.

As I wait for him to continue, the blood running through my veins seems to be lowering in temperature.

"Okay, you know me too well, brother," Abbott says.

"I'm still waiting for an explanation," I point out.

"Well, the thing is that, as you probably suspected, I have a bit of an ulterior motive in talking to you about the deal."

"I figured as much," I say, even though I hoped that it wasn't the case.

"The thing is that, brother..."

Abbott refers to me as brother instead of using my real name when he's trying to make a point, to influence me, to show his power.

I inhale deeply to gather my strength to withstand whatever he's about to throw at me.

"The thing is that you sort of have the one thing I want...and I just can't have that."

I know exactly what or rather who he's referring to before he can even say her name.

Everly.

He wants Everly.

My blood drops another degree.

Shivers run up my arms and make my hair stand up on end.

I don't want him even thinking about her, let alone saying her name out loud.

And the thought of anything more than that? I clench my fists in anger.

"The thing is that I want Everly, and I will do anything in my power to get her."

"You can't have her," I hiss. "She's mine."

"Not for long," Abbott starts to laugh again. I watch as his body seems to gather strength from his laughter, expanding his shoulders and widening his stance.

"Fuck you."

"No, but I'll definitely fuck her."

I want to launch myself at him, but something holds me back.

I'm a prisoner awaiting trial and he's the Prince of York.

I don't want to make my case any worse.

So, I clench my jaw and hold myself together.

"You know why I came here to talk to you?"

He's mocking me.

I don't respond.

"I think on some level I feel guilty for what I'm about to do. I wanted to give you a way out. Or at least, a way to bury yourself."

I narrow my eyes, not fully understanding what he's referring to.

"I'm about to ask Father for her hand in marriage."

CHAPTER 15 - EASTON

WHEN IT ALL TURNS TO BLACK...

I stare at him for a moment.

Did he really just say what I thought he said?

Everly?

He wants to marry my Everly?

"Everly! Everly!" he says, as if he can read my mind. "I'm going to marry *your* Everly!"

"No," I say, shaking my head. He narrows his eyes and begins to laugh.

"You're too smart for me, Easton."

This time his voice is low and thunderous, the one that is all too familiar to me.

"I thought I would come to you with this deal and I thought that you would jump at the chance to take it."

"Why the fuck would I plead guilty to something I didn't do?"

"I don't know, maybe because two years is better than a lifetime."

"I didn't kill him. And I'm going to prove that at trial."

"Oh, my dear, brother. You are still so naive, even after so many years of living in York. How is it that you are still so innocent?"

I shake my head.

"First of all, trials are not for proving innocence. They can only find you guilty or not guilty. And trust me, they will find you guilty."

"But I didn't do it," I insist.

"That doesn't matter." He laughs again. "But if it's any consolation, I believe you."

It's not. At this point, I care very little about what he believes.

"Don't you want to know how it is that I know what I know?"

"No, not really."

"Oh, c'mon, don't pretend. You do! You do want to know!" Abbott is mocking me.

He is practically dancing around me with anticipation.

It takes everything within me to keep my fists to myself.

Out of the corner of my eyes, I can see that the guards are watching.

He leans over to me.

He's so close that I can feel his breath on my skin.

I pull away from him, but he grabs my shirt and pulls me in for an embrace.

"I know because..." he whispers into my ear, "I did it."

I look at him, confused.

A large, wide smile full of satisfaction spreads across his face.

"I did it, Easton. I killed Dagger. I'll spare you the details, but I've been meaning to do it for some time now. You know Father, he put too much trust into him and Dagger didn't have much love for me. I couldn't have that. I thought that they would frame some innocent chap for the whole thing, little did I know that this thing would kill two birds with one stone, so to speak."

"Two birds?" I ask quietly, still trying to process everything that he had said to me.

"Well, you know, get rid of Dagger and get rid of *you*."

"Me? Why would you want to get rid of me?"

"I never did actually," Abbott says.

His tone changes again, reminding me of some of our better times. "We were never close, but I did have some affection for you. But then this business with Everly came about."

I hate the sound of her name in his mouth.

My fists ball up again against my wishes.

"Father was getting a little too excited for you two to marry. He was talking about you moving down here. Reconnecting. Like I said, Father is getting old and he might be becoming senile."

My eyes glaze over as I continue to stand here and listen to his speech.

"I don't know what's in store for him in the future, but I know what I'm owed. I will be the next King of York, Easton."

"What have I ever done to show you that I had any intentions of claiming that title? That's the last thing I want," I finally say. Suddenly, I feel like this whole thing is one big misunderstanding. Did he really think that I wanted anything to do with being the new King of York?

"You never said anything, but I didn't know if that meant anything. You play your cards close to the chest."

I shake my head and take a few steps to the side.

I take a deep breath and decide to try a tactic of compassion.

I'm not pleading for anything, but I'm trying to explain myself.

At least, tell him the truth.

Perhaps, then...I don't know. I have to give it a shot.

"All I want to do is marry Everly and get the fuck away from here," I say. "That's it. If we can leave today, we will. I want nothing to do with this place or its riches or its titles. You can have it all."

Abbott doesn't say anything for a moment.

"You want nothing to do with this place?" he asks.

My hopes rise a little bit.

Does he actually believe me?

Then maybe, just maybe...I don't dare finish the thought out of fear of cursing myself.

"Are you seriously saying that you are willing to abdicate the throne?" Abbott asks.

"I never had any intentions for the throne. I never wanted it," I say. "You can have it."

Abbott paces around the room for a moment, considering my offer. It's not so much of an offer as a plea.

"So, let me get this straight, you are willing to just walk away from your inheritance and your wealth and everything else you're entitled to as the Prince of York?"

I nod, quickly.

"And why is that?"

I shrug. "Because I never wanted it. I never thought it belonged to me. You are the one who deserves to sit on that throne, Abbott. Not me."

"Well, that's true."

Is this working?

Is my flattery actually making an impact?

"There is one other thing I deserve, though," Abbott says.

My chest tightens up.

I know what he is about to say before he says it.

I look into his eyes and suddenly everything that he has been doing here dawns on me.

CHAPTER 16 - EASTON

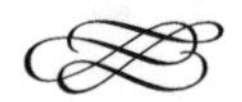

WHEN I CAN'T STAND IT ANYMORE...

Abbott was never going to give me a chance.

This was just a game.

Another one of his *fucking* games.

He looks me straight in the eye.

Without missing a beat he says,

"Everly is going to be my wife."

Before Abbott is even able to finish the sentence, I lunge at him.

I'm propelled more by the anger from somewhere deep within me than by actual force.

I land right on top of him and pound my fists into his face.

He will not say her name.

He will not touch her.

He will not do anything to harm a hair on her head.

The next few minutes are a daze of punches and hurt.

Our fists fly through the air and collide with our bodies.

At first, my hands throb with each collision, but after a while all of the pain goes away and is instead replaced with numbness.

Everything starts to move in slow motion.

I lose all feeling in my fists, but that feeling somehow spreads throughout my body like a wave.

One moment I'm on top of him, and the next I'm underneath.

His blows hit my head and chest and stomach.

I contract and shield myself and then I fight back.

My blows land on his ear and his face.

After a while, I don't know where his body ends and mine begins.

We continue to grapple and fight and pound into each other until the guards pull us away.

Mainly, they pull me away and then allow Abbott to get a few more blows in.

They hold me by my arms as he squares off with me and punches me straight in my face.

I can't protect myself.

All I can do is brace for impact.

One punch.

Another.

Everything gets blurry again.

And then it turns to black.

SOMETHING cold and wet hits my face and I manage to open my eyes through the slits that they've become.

My mouth is filled with the taste of iron.

Blood.

I spit some of it out onto the floor.

My lip is much fatter than I thought it would be, so it doesn't so much land onto the tile as it does ooze out of my mouth and onto my shirt.

"You're such an asshole, Easton!" Abbott yells, grabbing me by my shirt. "We could've been friends, you know? The way that brothers had to be. But you just wouldn't. You wouldn't let me teach you how to be in the world. You had to fight me the whole way."

What is he talking about?

My head buzzes so loudly that I can barely make out the words, let alone process them.

"There was a time I thought we could be friends," he continues his rant. "But you just... wouldn't conform. Why the fuck are you like this, Easton?"

"Wouldn't conform?" I ask, trying to stand up on my feet.

But after all of those blows to my head, my legs are weak, and I trip.

The guards holding me back try to prop me up without much success.

"I wouldn't conform to what exactly? This *fucking* place? This sadist island where men can do whatever they want to women? Without any consequences. No, actually, it's worse than that. Not only are there no consequences, there's praise. If you are an asshole and a dick and an abuser like you, you get a pass. You get elevated in life. But me, what do I get? I get sent to prison for a crime I didn't commit, that's what."

Abbott starts to laugh. "Don't you get it? After all of this time? Don't you get it?"

"What? Get what?"

"Father's theory about the world. You see, he created this place in his image. It's the way the outside world should be, according to him."

He laughs again and shakes his head in disbelief.

I have no idea what he's talking about, but I'm done talking.

"Women aren't like this," he says, getting completely serious and stern. "They are our property. Out there in the so-called real world, they are fighting for their rights. They are standing up to their abusers or whatever the fuck. But the thing is they don't deserve any rights. They aren't like us and they never will be."

He spits blood onto the floor as he says that.

I shake my head and broaden my shoulders.

What a piece of shit.

I always knew that there was something wrong with him, but I never knew how fucked up he really was.

There are things I can say to fight him on this, of course.

Like what about our mother?

She's a woman.

Didn't he love her?

Does he actually think she shouldn't have had any rights?

That she should've been our father's property.

But what would be the point?

I'm done talking to him.

Once and for all.

"What, you've got nothing to say?" Abbott taunts me. I shrug. "Are you seriously going to give me the silent treatment now?"

I shrug again.

He throws a light punch into my shoulder, egging me on.

"Okay then, that's fine. How about I leave you with this...I'm going to ask Father if I can marry Everly and he's going to agree."

My blood runs cold. I clench my jaw.

"I've never shown an interest in having a wife before and he'll be only too happy to oblige."

"Why?" I whisper.

"Why? 'Cause I like her. She's fight and she has heart. She fights hard. It's difficult to find a woman like that. A woman like that is wasted on you."

I try to push my way out of the guards' grasp, but they tighten their grip.

"And when we are married, she will be mine to do with what I want for as long as I want. And you've seen nothing yet."

A rush of anger from deep inside of me comes to the surface and I break free from the guards' grasp.

I launch my body on top of Abbott's, pushing him down to the floor.

I punch him in the face over and over again as fast as I can until the guards pull me off him.

He didn't see me coming and he looks dazed and bloodied by the attack.

The guards hit me in the stomach with their batons and push me toward the door.

Just as we're about to exit, Abbott runs up to me and pushes himself closer to my ear.

"You are going away, brother. For a long, long time. And as you sit in that cell all alone for years to come, for a crime you didn't commit, you will think of all the things I'm doing to your pretty girl. Better yet, I'll send you some pictures and videos to keep you occupied and I'll make sure that the guards make you watch them. 'Cause I want you to know just how much she's going to suffer in my hands. And just how much I hate you."

CHAPTER 17 - EASTON

WHEN I'M ALONE...

When they take me back to my cell, I am covered in blood and my fists are throbbing. I pace around like a caged animal.

My thoughts are completely focused on Abbott and everything that I'm going to do to him.

The punches he received just now aren't enough.

Nowhere near enough.

I just need the opportunity to throw one big one.

The kind that would knock him out for good.

Once and for all.

One punch homicide.

A man can dream, at least.

Unfortunately, I doubt that I will have the opportunity.

Abbott had laid it all on the line and he had

made threats against Everly.

He's a lot of things, but he is also a man of his word.

What he says he will do to Everly, he will likely do to her.

My fists ball up in anger and I throw one at the wall.

Luckily, I take a step back just in time before I make contact.

My knuckles are already bloody and worn, and a collision with the wall would surely break my hand.

No, he's not worth that. I swing through the air again, trying to calm myself down.

A nurse comes in to take a look at me.

She bandages me up and gives me some pills for the pain.

Advil, nothing too exciting.

She asks me questions about how I'm feeling, but I'm too wired to carry on a conversation.

And then something occurs to me.

"Everly, do you know, Everly?" I ask.

She looks into my eyes.

Her skin is lined and older, but her eyes twinkle as if they belong to a teenager.

"Everyone knows Everly," she says quietly.

"You have to warn her. You have to tell her what

Abbott intends to do," I plead.

She may be a House of York loyal or she might be a rebel.

I have no idea where her loyalties lie, but I have to try.

I have to reach out. I don't really have anything else to lose.

"I will warn her," the nurse says, pushing her dark hair out of her face. "But I have a feeling she already knows what's coming."

"You have to help her," I whisper. "You have to help her run away. She can't stay here anymore."

"This is an island, sir. There's nowhere to go."

"That's why you have to help her. There are boats and planes. People do get off this island, but they need friends."

The nurse shakes her head.

"Please," I plead.

"I can lie to you and say that I will," she says with a deep exhale, "but you will know as well as I do that that's an impossible thing to ask."

I know.

It's unfair.

It would put her life in danger.

If she is caught...she would be sent away to a labor camp or worse.

Yet, I have to ask.

For Everly's sake.

"As much as I want to help her, I can't risk it. I have a family."

She leaves shortly after as I slump into my bed and close my eyes.

A sense of helplessness fills the air and feels like it's choking me.

I can't breathe.

My throat is closing up.

I take it one breath at a time and continue to breathe despite everything.

The hours turn into days.

At first, I try to talk to the guards.

I ask them questions about my case and trial.

I wait and ask again.

But it's all to no avail.

They don't respond, and I ask less and less.

Mainly, I just wait.

I sit on the bed and wait. I lie on the bed and wait.

I wait until I can't wait anymore and then I wait some more.

I don't know when my trial will be, and I don't know when I can see Tiger again. I don't know if there will be any consequences for attacking Abbott.

Here in my cell, in which I spend twenty-four hours a day, I don't know anything about the outside world.

The one thing that is different from before is that I am no longer taken out for exercise.

Now, even that privilege has been revoked.

Now, I'm just alone with my thoughts all day and all night.

When you are alone all the time, you have a lot of time to think.

But it's not so much thinking as dwelling.

I don't have the power to change anything, so I just sit here and steep in my regrets.

And with regret, comes another thought.

It's quiet at first, sitting in the back of your mind as a possibility.

And then with each passing day, it creeps closer and closer until it's the only thing you can think about.

My own death.

I don't have the power to do much, but I do have the power to orchestrate that. I have bed sheets.

I have a bed with a metal frame.

And suddenly, just like that, all I can think about is how much better off I'd be if I weren't here anymore.

Perhaps, Abbott would lose interest in Everly.

Perhaps, Father would realize that I had nothing to do with Dagger's death.

If nothing else, I doubt that anyone would miss me anyway.

And there's that other thought; the sweet relief of death.

At least I wouldn't have to wait for the inevitable anymore. I can take it into my own hands and end it once and for all.

"Come on, get up!" A loud voice breaks my concentration. "Get up!"

I do as I am told.

I put my hands through the slot in the door and let them put handcuffs on me.

They don't put the shackles around my legs and I revel in the little bit of freedom this allows me.

Then they open the door and walk me down a long hallway I haven't seen in who knows how long.

"Where are we going?" I ask.

Is the trial starting?

Are they taking me to see Tiger again?

Is the trial beginning?

Or am I finally going out to the exercise yard again?

"You'll see."

PART FOUR

CHAPTER 18 - EVERLY

WHEN I'M ALONE...

I have not heard anything about Easton in days.

Not since that fight he had with Abbott.

I haven't seen him since the arrest, but the whole mansion is just seeping in gossip over what happened.

All video recording was turned off, so that makes the rumors even more intense and potent.

The guards could only hear a little bit and who knows if what they relayed was even true?

I had my doubts about the whole story in general, until I saw Abbott's face.

It was a few days after, and his eyes were still like slits.

His whole face was black and blue as if he had been beaten to a pulp.

It took all of my willpower to keep the smile that was rising within from escaping my lips.

Easton had beaten him up.

He had hurt him and now he was in pain.

At least, there has been some retribution for all the evil that Abbott has imparted on the world.

When I saw Abbott's face, it was only out of the corner of my eye.

After being an almost constant presence in the house, flirting with Olivia and Savannah and even me, he practically disappeared after his fight with Easton.

And when I did see him again?

It was completely by accident.

I was going on a walk with Teal and he had just hopped into a brand new, red Ferrari. I don't know much about cars, but Teal's brother is really into them so she educated me.

Though the car was nice to look at, what I really enjoyed was looking at Abbott's bruised face.

I saw him for only a moment, but I relished in the gruesomeness that Easton had imparted on him for days after.

But, besides this one encounter, my days here at

the house after Easton's arrest have been quite uneventful.

The first night I worried that they would take me away, too, but Mirabelle came and eased my fears.

She promised that she would warn me if they were ever going to come for me and so far, after all of this week, no one has come.

Apparently, the powers that be have decided that Easton had acted alone.

So, for now, I spend my days doing what all the other girls are doing.

Lounging by the pool.

Reading.

Going on walks by the beach.

The guards continue to watch us pretty closely and there are places around the property that are off limits, but other than that, I have a lot more freedom than I did before.

The doors aren't locked.

I can come and go as I please.

I even have access to the large library, which I lose myself in quite often.

There're only so many hours in the day that I can watch television and Netflix and I've always been more partial to books.

But besides making friends and growing closer

to the girls here, there's one other thing I do to occupy my time.

I wait.

I learn and watch and search, but mostly I wait.

I have explored the area in quite a lot of detail, hence the need to take so many walks. And now I feel like I'm pretty familiar with it.

I can get around, but I still don't see a way out.

York is an island and an island doesn't need to have much protection or guards since it's surrounded completely by water.

Water is a natural barrier.

There are also no boats anywhere near the water and there are no bridges connecting the island to anything else.

On my walks, I have explored most of it quite carefully and I have discovered that this place is like a fortress.

No one comes in or out of it without someone else's permission.

No wonder they have no issues with me wandering around the place.

There's nowhere to go.

Or is there?

I have to keep hope alive.

The thing that gave me the strength to make it through those nights of total darkness was hope.

Hope is all you have sometimes and it's everything.

Without it, you would be lost and with it, you have a reason to keep trying.

My life in the House of York isn't nearly as bad now as it was then.

There are dark clouds looming up ahead, of course, but for now, life is fine.

Good.

Comfortable.

That's more than I've had before and for that I am grateful.

What does the future hold?

I don't know exactly but I know the rumors.

Abbott has his eye on me.

He has me in his crosshairs.

I don't know what's going to happen at Easton's trial, but the gossip has been swirling out of control ever since their fight.

Some people are saying that Easton is going to be found guilty for sure, but others are holding out hope.

Almost no one thinks that Easton actually did it, or maybe that's just something they're saying to me?

York is a place of secrets and agendas, which makes it hard to decipher what's true and what's not.

When I am not outside, wandering the grounds, or hanging out with the girls, I'm usually in my room.

I need the time to decompress and relax.

I lie down on the large king-size bed and bury my head in a book.

* * *

I'M READING three or four books a week now, mainly because I need to escape. And burying my head in a book allows me to do just that.

There's something so relaxing about reading about other people's problems rather than living in your own.

A knock on the door startles me and I look up from my book.

With the pillows propped up just so behind my back and under my knees, it takes me a moment to actually see who it is.

"Everly," Mirabelle says and walks up to me.

I've gotten pretty close to Mirabelle and I appreciate her candor and openness.

When there are things that she can't talk about,

instead of simply lying she simply says that it's not something she can discuss.

That kind of honesty is difficult to find.

"What's up?" I ask, putting the bookmark in to not lose my spot.

"They have a surprise for you."

CHAPTER 19 - EVERLY

WHEN SHE HAS A SURPRISE...

Wait, a second.

What kind of surprise?

Good? Bad?

I demand to know more, but Mirabelle just repeats herself.

I understand the words, but not their implication.

"Why can't you tell me?" I ask.

"I just can't. Get ready."

"Now?"

She nods.

I stare at her.

I'm wearing jeans and a t-shirt and flip-flops.

I am ready in that I'm dressed, but I don't know if I'm dressed for this since I don't know what this is.

"Never mind, you look fine. Follow me."

I do as she says.

But as I follow her, I throw out more questions at her. Questions that she doesn't answer.

When it seems like she's finally exhausted by me, she stops and turns toward me.

"Look, I don't know what's going on. I have no idea what they're doing..."

The last bit of the sentence comes out softer than the rest.

She's right.

Of course, she's right.

My heart beats loudly.

Each step I take, my head gets flooded with blood and I can barely hear my own thoughts.

Mirabelle leads me out of the main mansion and toward the King's house.

In all of my explorations, I've stayed away from this place because I was told to stay away.

But I know the rumors.

The dungeons, where they kept me and many others are underground.

Is that where they're keeping him?

But instead of heading downstairs down to the basement, Mirabelle makes a turn down a wide hallway with linoleum flooring.

The walls are taupe and have the distinct look of an institution to them.

In fact, they remind me of my middle school. Same dull lighting without a window in sight.

Same flooring which makes a loud sneaking sound when you scruff your feet.

The only difference is that there are no motivational posters on the walls reminding you that you are different from everyone else.

One large hall becomes a smaller waiting room and then an even smaller room.

When we finally reach this small room, Mirabelle says that she is going to leave me here.

"What is this room?" I ask.

There's a large window in the middle with a view of the water.

But the window doesn't open; it's a bay window like the kind they have in hotels.

The room is quite small, about the size of a doctor's examination room.

There's a mid-century modern fabric, low-profile couch next to one wall with a matching coffee table in front of it and two gray chairs on opposite ends.

The decor of the room is warm and modern and Scandinavian.

Wealthy without being ostentatious.

Functional and comfortable.

I look around the room carefully, noting that there are no cameras.

At least, no visible ones.

When I look back from the window, Mirabelle is about to leave.

"Where are you going?" I ask.

"You don't want me here for this."

"For what?"

She gives me a small, mysterious smile out of the corner of her lips and disappears behind the door.

However unusual this is, it is probably not something I should be too concerned about.

I trust Mirabelle.

If whatever awaits me here is going to be bad, she'd warn me. I'm sure of it.

I nod, trying to convince myself further. I do trust Mirabelle, but this is York.

This place is full of surprises.

So, my trust in her has its limits.

But I don't think she would outwardly deceive me like this.

I walk around the room and look out of the floor-to-ceiling window. It's a few floors up and I'm at about eye level with the top of the shorter palm trees.

I look down at the waves and how slow they are in their crashes.

Delicate.

Yet deliberate.

They are small, but fierce and unstoppable.

The sky above is full of puffy clouds which hang low in the sky. The sun's rays break through around the edges, giving the sky an effervescent glow.

A knock at the door sends my heart into my throat.

I'm more scared than I thought.

Who am I going to see on the other side?

I refuse to let his name pop into my head, but sometimes our thoughts get the best of us.

What if it's Abbott?

What if he's here to have a private conversation with me?

I look around the room for a sharp object or an escape plan.

I kick myself for not looking for either earlier.

And now it's too late.

Another knock on the door.

"Come in!" I say, reluctantly.

My voice cracks in the middle. I clear my throat.

The door swings open.

It's *him*.

A lump forms in the back of my throat, the kind that sends tears streaming down my face.

He runs up to me and takes me into his arms.

He whispers something into my ear, but I can't quite make out any of it.

I wrap my arms around him and bury my head in his chest.

Then he lifts up my chin and places his lips onto mine.

CHAPTER 20 - EVERLY

WHEN I CAN'T BELIEVE IT…

It takes a while for us to pull away from one another.

We lose ourselves in each other's arms and spend a few minutes just running our arms around each other's bodies.

Is this real?

Am I really touching Easton?

Is he really touching me?

All the contact doesn't go far.

The clothes stay on, but my thoughts continue to wander. I haven't seen or smelled or touched or been near Easton for so long that I feel feverish.

It's like I've been on a diet and finally I'm allowed to binge. It's a crude analogy, I know, but it's how I feel.

I want him.

I crave him.

Now, that I finally have him here, all alone, I want to take him into my arms and do dirty things to him.

And I want him to do dirtier things to me.

Probably, feeling the same way that I'm feeling, starved for love, Easton starts to nibble on my earlobe and then kisses me up and down my neck.

I tilt my head back in pleasure.

My legs open on their own accord.

He runs his hands down my thighs and I run mine on top of his pants. He is hard and welcoming, calling me to him.

I'm about to climb on top of him, when I suddenly pull away.

Tears again start to run down my face.

I'm so overwhelmed with emotion that I can't seem to get ahold of myself.

"I'm so sorry," I whisper.

Without asking me to explain, Easton takes me into his arms and cradles me.

"Why are you sorry?" he asks over and over.

As tears stream down my face, I tell him how much I'm just sorry for everything that has happened.

"You don't deserve to be here. This isn't fair."

He gives me a shrug and wraps his arms tighter around me.

I cry, and cry and I feel stupid and silly for crying, but then I cry some more.

I know that my tears are coming from exhaustion.

I am spent and tired and out of control.

Nothing in this place is mine and I don't have influence over anything.

I feel like a ping-pong, just bouncing against the walls, going with the flow of the force that's impacted on me.

But I'm not a plastic ball.

I'm a person, with feelings and emotions, and a sense of self.

At least, that's what I had before.

"I'm so sorry that I'm taking our time up with this," I say, brushing my tears off my cheeks with the back of my hands. "You really don't need this. I'm just feeling a bit...overwhelmed. Too emotional."

"It's okay. It's really okay. I'm here for you."

It takes me a few more minutes to gather my composure.

I wipe my eyes.

The tears feel good to come out; they are like a release of energy that has been stored up too long.

I wouldn't say that now, finding myself in his arms, I feel like I don't have to be strong anymore.

I don't believe that tears are a sign of weakness, but rather just being in touch with your feelings.

It's more like they are simply a release of all the negativity and sadness and helplessness that I've been storing inside of me for way too long.

After a few minutes, I wipe my eyes for the last time and no more tears emerge. Whatever needed to come out, came out and now I feel a bit more at peace.

"Are you okay?"

Yes, I nod.

Easton leans over and gives me another warm hug, perhaps for good measure.

"I missed you so much," I say. "How are you?"

We talk for a bit about how things are.

How he's feeling. Fine.

How they've been treating him. Fine.

He doesn't go into much detail and whatever he does say basically comes down to "I'm fine."

I don't believe him, but the more I press, the more he insists that he's fine.

"Listen, I don't really want to talk about that

here, you know? I mean, I'm being treated fine, but the trial is going to begin and then I don't know what's going to happen."

I can hear the fear in his voice.

I see it in his face as well.

I feel helpless to do anything about it.

So, instead I try to change the subject.

"Why do you think they brought us here? Together?"

He shrugs.

"I had no idea where they were taking me when they brought me here."

"Me either," I say.

He looks around the walls and the ceiling.

Then he gets up from the couch and picks up the lamp.

He flips it over in his hands and examines it closely. He does the same thing with the phone on the end table.

It's a typical hotel room phone, large, plastic: and filled with buttons, many of which are labeled.

"What are you doing?" I ask.

But instead of answering me, he flips the phone over and uses a pair of tweezers he found in the drawer to open the back.

Inside, there's just a mess of wires.

He looks them over carefully and then puts the plastic cover back on.

I ask him again, but again he doesn't respond, just giving me a small shake of the head. He continues to make his way around the room looking for something.

But what?

I sit on the couch and watch him unscrew every lightbulb and look under every device. When he's finally satisfied that he has searched the entire room completely, he comes back to the couch and sits down next to me.

"This room isn't bugged," he says.

I stare at him, unsure as to how I'm supposed to react to this.

"They are not recording what's happening here. They aren't even watching."

I shrug. "So, what does that mean?"

He looks at me confused and then opens his mouth to explain. But the the words don't come exactly.

"Well, um...I don't know exactly but it means something, right? I mean...it has to?"

I shrug. It does sound rather significant.

"Who do you think is responsible for bringing us here? I mean, in arranging this whole thing?" I ask.

Easton shrugs. "I've been trying to figure that out ever since I saw you here. But no one comes to mind. I mean, who would want us to be together?
And why?"

"Mirabelle?" I ask.

"Mirabelle!?" He shakes his head. "She's one of my father's oldest employees. She is nice, but she is very loyal to him."

"I don't know. She and I have gotten really close. I mean, she has been really kind to me. And she knew how heartbroken I was over this whole thing."

Easton nods.

I see him processing the information, but not really agreeing with my assessment.

"If it's not her, then who?"

He thinks about it for a moment. "Tiger."

I don't even know *what* that is.

"That's my attorney's name. Well, his nickname."

That still doesn't make sense to me, so Easton explains.

He tells me about Tiger and how he got the impression that he really wants to help him.

"But what would arranging this meeting accomplish?" I ask. "I mean, what's the point?"

Easton doesn't know the answer to that anymore than I do.

"Let's not worry about this," he says after a moment. "It doesn't matter."

"It does," I insist.

"Well, it does, but not that much. There's something else I want to do right now."

He pulls me closer to him and presses his lips onto mine.

PART FIVE

CHAPTER 21 - EASTON

WHEN THE WORLD FADES AWAY...

My hands make my way down her neck and toward the top of her breasts. As her breathing speeds up, I feel the way they rise up and fall down in uneven intervals.

I am torn between wanting to undress her and get inside of her as quickly as possible and extending this moment so that I can savor it and make it last.

As I kiss her, I open my eyes to see how she'd like for this to proceed.

But she seems lost in the moment.

I let my eyelids drop back down and decide to let the moment take me wherever it wants.

My hands make their way down her body.

Under her clothes, I feel the slimness of her waist.

I trail my fingertips across her thigh. Her legs open up to welcome me further and I accept.

When I tug at her pants to pull them off, she clenches her legs and my arms to stop me. But only for a moment.

Then she lets go and I continue.

I pull off my shirt and she runs her fingertips over my stomach, feeling the outline of each muscle.

I tighten my core to really give her something to grab onto and she sighs in response.

"You are so…hot."

I kiss underneath her earlobe and laugh a little at her lack of eloquence.

"You are pretty amazing yourself," I say, pulling off her top and bra.

I glance at the freckles around her body and take my lips down along each one, pausing for a kiss.

The pink of her nipples distracts me and when I press my lips to them, they harden against my tongue.

Her hair falls in natural waves around her body and it gets tangled up in my fists as I make my way down her body.

She runs her fingers down past my belly button.

I need her to touch me there, I need her to grab it, but she doesn't.

Instead, she circles back up and smiles.

"Are you teasing me?" I ask, climbing on top of her.

We are both nude now and whatever restraint I had before is all but gone.

"Just a little," she jokes.

I push her shoulders down with my hands and take pleasure in her little moan.

My body drapes over hers and now she's so small under me that I can barely see her at all.

But I feel her.

Her hands on my skin.

Her fingernails digging into my shoulder blades.

Her moaning below me.

Her saying my name.

Her legs open up and she welcomes me inside.

I thrust myself into her as she pulls me closer.

My hands get tangled up in her hair as I cradle her head and kiss her neck.

She licks my lips and moans louder into my ear.

I run my hands down her body, giving her butt a little pat.

This prompts her to grab my butt cheeks with

both hands and squeeze them with all of her strength.

We start to move as one.

One motion.

Riding the same wave.

Our breathing matches the rhythm of our bodies and speeds up when we speed up. Her moans get louder and louder.

Her whispers of my name turn into yells. I can't hold on anymore.

When she yells my name at the top of her lungs and falls limply under me, I start to move my pelvis faster and faster.

And then, suddenly, all tension reaches a climax and then, poof. It vanishes from my body.

Whatever energy was propelling me all this time goes away with it.

I lower myself down on top of her and close my eyes.

"I love you."

"I love you, too," Everly whispers.

CHAPTER 22 - EVERLY

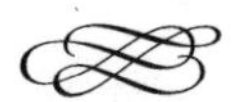

WHEN WE'RE ALONE...

Lying in the afterglow of what happened in his arms, I feel myself relaxing and floating away.

Never in a million years did I think that they would let us do this, yet here we are.

And for a brief moment, my mind isn't occupied with all the questions about why and how, but rather with simply enjoying the moment.

Easton rubs my shoulders and plays with my hair, without saying a word.

I don't know how much time passes as we simply lie here.

Alone.

Together.

The way it's supposed to be.

"Do you ever think what our life together would be out there?" I finally ask.

"All the time."

"Me, too."

"What do you think it will be like?" he asks.

I think about it for a moment.

My ideal life? That's hard to imagine from York.

"I just want to take you back home," I finally say. "I want to show you my tiny apartment and I want to be there with you."

He nods.

"Before I got here, I was really not grateful for what I had. I mean, I had this job that I thought was pretty boring. I didn't know what I wanted to do with my life. I felt like everyone was living this amazing life but me. And now? Now, I realize that I all need in my life to make me happy is you."

Easton laughs.

"Well, no, not really. But you know what I mean."

He shakes his head.

"I may still not want to go back to my old job, but I would be grateful just to not be here anymore. That would be enough. And if I could be back there in my apartment with you...my life would be pretty perfect."

Easton nods and kisses the top of my head.

"All I need is you," he finally says. "I've seen what all this power and money can bring and I don't want any of it. Maybe there's another way to have it, but here on York, it comes with a lot of blood on your hands."

I nod.

"I just want to go somewhere and start my life with you. I don't care where as long as it's far, far away from here."

We lie in silence for a moment, trying to imagine what that would be like. To not be here anymore. But then my thoughts quickly drift back to reality.

"What's going to happen with the trial?" I ask.

"I have a good lawyer. At least, I think he's good. I guess he'll do his best."

"You really think that your father will want you to go trial? I mean, he really thinks you killed Dagger?"

Easton nods. "Don't you?"

"No," I say, shaking my head.

I've had my doubts before, but looking at him now, I am certain of the fact that he's innocent.

Even if he had cause, and it would've been justified, I'm certain that he did not kill him. I know it's not very scientific.

I know that it's just a feeling.

But sometimes, a feeling is all you have.

Sometimes, it's all you need.

As we talk more about the upcoming trial, Easton starts to get more distant. His demeanor changes and he even physically pulls away from me.

"I'm here for you," I say. "No matter what."

"That's exactly what I'm worried about."

"I don't understand," I say, shaking my head.

"There may come a time, when you shouldn't be here for me anymore. They are framing me for this crime, and they're going to get away with it. I'm certain of it."

"Don't say that," I whisper.

Tears start to well up.

"I'm telling you this, because they're going to make you choose, Everly. They're going to make you choose between right and wrong. Between me and York. They will test your allegiance."

"My allegiance is with you."

He shakes his head. "No, it can't be. Not if you want to stay safe."

"I don't care about that," I say. "All I want to do is be with you."

Easton pulls away from me and squares himself. His shoulders are across from mine and he looks deep into my eyes.

"You have to listen to me, Everly. I love you. Nothing is going to change that. I want you to be my wife. But if this trial goes forward, which I know it will, they will find me guilty. And then they will ask you to choose. Will you stand with a guilty man accused of betraying his home and the King, or will you stand with York?"

My whole body begins to shake.

It starts with my shoulders and spreads throughout my body.

The quivers quickly turn into an earthquake and suddenly I'm completely unable to control any part of me.

Tears stream down my face and my hands tremble as I reach for his face.

Easton shakes me to snap me out of the trance, but it's to no avail.

"You cannot stand by my side, Everly. You have to denounce me and our relationship. You have to pledge your allegiance to York. You have to say that I'm guilty. Whatever you do, you cannot fight them on this."

I continue to shake and cry and he wraps his arms around me and buries my head in his shoulders.

"I know it will be hard. But you have to survive,

Everly. No matter, what you do. You have to survive."

"Why?" I mumble through my sobs. "What's the fucking point?"

"Because as long as I'm alive, I will do everything in my power to come back for you. No matter how long it takes, Everly. No matter what they do to me. I will never forget you and I will be there for you."

The words echo in my mind, but I don't really process them.

Yet, Easton keeps trying to make them stick.

"You have to stay alive, Everly. No matter what happens, please promise me that."

I look up at him.

His face looks crestfallen and tired, but his eyes are full of fire and rage.

"They're going to marry you off to Abbott. He wants you and when I'm found guilty, he will get you. My father will see to it."

I shake my head again, but he puts his hands around my ears and physically stops me.

"Please, do as he says, whatever he says," Easton pleads.

"Why? What's the point of this anyway?"

"Because then, at least, you will still be...alive."

Of course, I know that the threat of my death is

there, but I haven't felt it be so close to me until this very moment.

I thought that getting out of the dungeon was enough. I thought that winning the competition was enough.

But it's not.

Not even close.

Now, there are more games to play.

My only concern is that I don't think I have the strength anymore.

Not after this.

CHAPTER 23 - EASTON

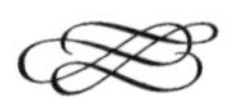

WHEN WE'RE ALONE...

As I hold her close to me, my thoughts meander around and focus on one thing.

The only thing that really scares me: the world without Everly in it.

What will happen to her if I'm found guilty?

No, not if, when.

Despite Tiger's best intentions and efforts, I am pretty certain that the reason that she's here now is to say goodbye.

I don't know who arranged this meeting, but it probably means that whatever is about to come about from the trial is not going to be good.

And what then?

The trial will come and go.

They will present their witnesses.

They will have their testimony. Most will lie, I'm sure. I'll tell the truth, and no one will believe me.

It will be a play put on to appease my father and brother. They will finally have a reason to put me away.

Lock me away in Hamilton or another labor prison, never to be heard from again.

I know that now.

I know that unless I can find some way to escape that will be my fate. But what about Everly?

What will become of her?

Abbott.

The thought of him makes my blood run cold.

He wants her and after I'm convicted, he will get her.

He will ask for her hand in marriage and my father will allow it.

And then she will be his to do with what he wants.

How long will Everly last like that?

I can see it in her eyes, and that her fire is flickering.

She believes that everything's going to be okay, and I want her to believe that for as long as possible.

Hope is sometimes all we can hold on to, because it's the only fuel we have.

"If you are convicted and they marry me off to him, I won't last long," she says quietly.

My hands are buried in her hair.

She says the words in a despondent manner.

She's resigned.

It's almost as if she's at peace with it.

I know what she means without her having to say it, but I need to know that what I know is right.

"What do you mean?"

"You know what I mean."

"No, I don't," I lie.

"I'm going to kill myself, Easton."

The words hang in the air between us.

It's my worst nightmare.

I shake my head and this time tears start to well up in my eyes.

She looks at me, but does not flinch.

"You can't."

"You won't be there to stop me."

"Please don't."

She shakes her head. "What would be the point? To live my life in captivity? To be raped? To be demeaned? To never see you again?"

"I'll come back for you, as long as I have breath in me, I will."

She shakes her head.

"You don't believe me?"

"I do believe you. At least, I know you'll try."

"Isn't that enough?" I ask.

She shakes her head.

"I've been through so much here, Easton. And it has been hell. The only thing that has made it even a little good is you. And now…if they take you away from me, what would be the fucking point? What would be the point of living?"

"Because maybe things will change in the future. My father might die and things might get better for you. Abbott might become interested in someone else. Life is long, Everly. Lots of things can happen. Taking your own life is so…final. There's no coming back from that."

She listens to me, but I don't know if she can hear me.

I also don't know if I'm asking something impossible from her.

I don't know the depths of the pain that she has felt.

I don't know the horror that she has been through.

All I know is that she does not want to go through that again.

"I know how unfair I'm being asking you this, but I can't imagine my life without you."

"You are going to live your life without me," she says.

"I can't imagine living in a world without you."

She nods and looks away.

"Do you think that's why they arranged this meeting?" Everly asks after a moment. I don't want to answer her. She searches my face and I give her a nod.

Neither of us speak for a few moments.

The gravity of the situation is finally setting in.

What is going to happen after she leaves here?

What is going to happen to her?

What is going to happen to me?

We can't possibly know.

All we have is this moment right now.

"There's a small fleet of airplanes located on the south side of the island."

She looks up at me, with a confused look on her face.

"You walk past what looks to be the beginning of a jungle and keep going. Just keep walking and walking and then you'll see a small air strip. The ground has been cleared of trees and the grass is mowed, or is mowed occasionally. It doesn't look like much, but it's enough for all of those planes to take off."

"Why are you telling me this?"

"Because you have to know. It's the only way off the island.

"There's a guard there, or two, but that's it. It's not as closely watched as the rest of the place because it's pretty well hidden."

"I don't know how to fly."

"I do."

She stares at me, dumbfounded.

"I finished pilot school and I'm about halfway through my hours to get the license. It was just a hobby of mine. But that doesn't matter. What matters is the guard, whose name is Daniel, is a friend of mine. A close friend. He owes me a favor. And he knows how to fly."

Everly shakes her head in disbelief.

"You have to make your way down there," I continue. "You have to ask him to fly you out. He knows about my arrest. And his family lives off the island. I will give you the number to a private bank account I have. It has almost two million dollars in it. From it, you will pay him two-hundred thousand dollars for helping you. But only after you are safe, with a new identity."

She nods, taking it all in.

And then she looks up at me and asks, "So, if you had this way off the island, why didn't you leave before?"

CHAPTER 24 - EASTON

WHEN WE'RE ALONE...

Her question echoes in my mind.

If I knew how to get off the island, why didn't I?

Why didn't I just take her and go?

Why didn't I just leave everything behind?

That question is something I've toyed with ever since I got here.

I should have.

I know that now.

But to do so was to cut ties with everyone. For good. It's not that I didn't want to. I did. Of course, I did.

Perhaps, the answer is that I thought that I had more time.

I needed time to exact my revenge. I needed time to plan for my father's downfall for killing Alicia.

But the real answer is that I was greedy.

"I'm sorry," I say after a long pause. "I thought everything was going well. My father was even going to let us get married. I thought that I had more time to avenge her death and avenge everything else that my father and brother have done. And now...it's too late."

Everly nods and looks away.

"What if it's not?"

"What do you mean?" I ask.

"What if it's not too late for us to get away? What if we could somehow escape from here?"

"Then...things would be different."

"I'm going to try," she says. Her eyes light up with excitement. There's that glimmer of hope. It took her from the brink of suicide to the beginning of a new life. I don't want to squash it, but I don't want her to risk her life in trying to fix something unfixable.

"This place is a jail. An actual jail," I say. "There's no way out."

"But we have to try. We have to do something."

"We are going to do something. You are. You are going to leave me and head to the air strip and you're going to escape. Now, listen to me."

I lean over and whisper the number of my bank account into her ear.

I also give her the pin, the routing number and the secret password, which will allow her to withdraw money without my presence.

The money's in a Caribbean bank which goes out of its way to protect the privacy of its users, but is also well aware of the fact that its users may require a stranger to withdraw the funds at a moment's notice.

The fact that my father's companies have no reach there was one of the main reasons I'd decided to go with it over its competitors.

"Repeat the numbers back to me," I say, and she does.

She does and stumbles.

Then she stumbles again.

We keep going until they are crystal clear in her mind and then I ask her to repeat them three more times.

After she has them memorized, Everly again tries to convince me that there's some way to escape from here and that she's going to find it.

"No," I say categorically. "You will do no such thing. It's too dangerous. The only advantage you have now is that they don't suspect that you might be a flight risk. Not yet. Not before my trial starts. So, this is the only time you have to go."

"I can't just leave you here," she pleads.

But my mind is made up.

"Once you are free, out there, with all that money to get yourself a new identity, then and only then can you look into helping me. But you will have to be very careful and you will need to hire professional help."

I whisper another few names into her ear.

They belong to people I've heard of, who have experience in these matters.

Well, not these matters exactly, but in extracting people from war zones and other difficult situations.

Everly is shaking her head, but I can see that I'm finally getting to her.

"I've given this a lot of thought. It's the only way we can both get out of here. It's the only way you can actually help me, Everly. Please do this."

After a few moments, she gives me a little nod and wraps her arms tightly around me.

I hear footsteps somewhere outside the door.

We don't have much time.

I need her to promise me this now.

"Will you do this?" I ask, my voice cracking with desperation.

She can lie, of course.

Just tell me what I want to hear, but something tells me she won't.

This is her chance to get off the island.

To escape and to actually have resources with which to help me.

"I don't know if I can," she says, shaking her head. "I'm scared."

Of all the things I've thought about, of all the reasons, it never occurred to me that this is one.

Fear.

It's a basic emotion we all have.

"You have been through so much, Everly. I know. It's hard. But if you don't do this, things will get worse. You know that."

"But what if Tiger comes through? What if everything turns out okay and they let us get married?"

I nod.

"That's possible, right? What if we just...wait?"

I'm not getting through to her and I don't have anymore time.

I hear voices coming from somewhere far away.

They are going to be here any moment.

"Everly, you can't wait. This is your chance. You have to find that air strip. You have to find Daniel.

He's a big guy with dark hair who sweats profusely. You have to get him to fly you off the island."

Grabbing her by the shoulders, I try to shake her out of her trance.

"You can NOT tell him how much money you have, but you have to convince him that you have enough for him to risk his job. You have to pay him two-hundred thousand because it is what he will need to disappear and keep his family safe."

"I don't want to hear this," she moans and tries to kiss me. But I pull away.

"No, you will listen to me. You will do this, Everly, otherwise you are a goner. You will be Abbott's and you will lose yourself here."

She shakes her head. The door starts to open.

"Do this for me. Please," I plead. "I need you to do this. It's the only way I'll ever get out of here."

The door swings open and I pull her close to me. The time to talk is over.

CHAPTER 25 - EASTON

WHEN THEY TAKE HER AWAY...

When they came for her, I didn't fight them on it.

It was a gift that I got to see her at all, let alone do anything else with her.

And now, the moment is over.

Now, it is time for her go.

The guards come in.

I give Everly a brief kiss on the lips. She kisses me back and that is it.

Will I ever see her again? I do not know.

All I know is that I want to, and that she has to make her way off this God forsaken island.

After she leaves, I expect them to take me back to my cell.

But they don't.

Instead, they lead me into the main house and toward my father's private chambers. I am shackled and tired, but I am here to see the king at his behest.

I wonder what he has to say to me.

The guards knock on the door and a servant answers.

They lead me inside.

My father is again sitting at his desk, reading a book. He does not look up.

"Leave us," he says. "Take off those handcuffs."

"But your Majesty..." the shorter one starts to protest, but my father simply raises his finger and he closes his mouth.

Using his key, he unlocks the cuffs around my wrists and then around my ankles.

"I'll call you when we're done," my father says and waves for them to leave.

I rub my wrists to get the blood flowing again.

"Thank you for that," I add.

I don't know what I'm doing here, so I wait patiently for my father to finish.

When I was young, this room used to elicit so much mystery and wonder from me.

It was full of thick books in which you could get lost for days.

I liked coming in here and curling up on the couch by the wall.

I liked picking a book from the shelf and listening as my father conducted his businesses.

What happened to this place? I wonder.

But the truth is that nothing happened. This place is exactly as it always was.

My father is exactly as he always was.

The only difference is that I have grown up.

The magic is gone.

And reality has set in.

The truth about who he is and what he's capable of is something that I am keenly aware of now.

"Thank you for coming to see me, Easton," my father says, as if I'm doing him a favor. I give him a brief nod.

"I hope that you are being treated well."

"I'm fine."

"Are the accommodations comfortable?"

"Decent. But given that I didn't do anything, I don't really know why I'm there."

My father looks up.

I had promised myself to keep my temper under control, but somehow the words escaped me.

I am not a very angry person, but my father brings out the worst in me.

"I did not kill him," I add. "I didn't kill, Dagger. You know that, right?"

"If I knew that, then you would not be on trial, son."

"You really think I killed him?"

"Dagger is dead."

"Yes, I know, but I didn't do it."

He glares at me. I glare back.

"You had every reason to."

I shake my head. "I might have wanted to, but I did not do it."

Now, it's my father's turn to shake his head. Does he really not believe me?

"What can I do to convince you?" I plead.

"There's going to be a trial, son, and a jury of your peers is going to decide."

All this time, I thought that this was a sham.

A show trial.

I thought that he had already convicted me.

Framed me.

But what if he really isn't sure?

"You're going to let them decide about my guilt or innocence?" I ask. "People you don't know. What's the point? You're the king."

"That's right. I am. And that's what I want."

I shake my head.

"Okay, you want to know the truth, Easton?"

I nod.

"I know you did it," he says, getting up from behind his desk. "I know you did it because I know that you know that I ordered Dagger to get rid of your little girlfriend. She was a distraction you didn't need. She wanted to get you away from this place. And she almost did."

There it is.

The truth.

The man that I had suspected my father to be, but hoped that he wasn't, is right here before me.

"You ordered him to kill her?" I whisper.

"C'mon, you knew that already. She was a bad influence. You didn't need her in your life."

"You never thought anyone was good enough for me."

"Now, let's get something straight. That's not true. I was actually quite excited about you marrying Everly. She's a smart girl. She knows how the game is played and she doesn't rock the boat. She would be a good match for you. Why do you think I arranged for that little meeting you just had with her? I don't do that for everyone, you know."

"So why aren't we getting married?" I ask.

My father takes a step toward me.

He is standing only a few inches away from me.

He is so close that I can feel his breath on my face.

"You killed my oldest friend, son. The one person who has been with me through everything. From the beginning of all of this. You took him away from me."

CHAPTER 26 - EASTON

WHEN I TRY TO GET HIM TO UNDERSTAND...

I take a step back, shaking my head.

How can I make him understand?

How can I convince him that I did not do this?

"You are right," I say. "You are right. I did want him dead. When I found out that you ordered him to kill her, I was angry and hurt and mad as hell. At you. And at him. I vowed revenge. I plotted. I tried to think of the best way to do it. But the time never came. You see, that's why I stayed here. That's why I kept staying here. I thought I could have more time. I thought that if I had just waited for it, the right moment would present itself."

My father nods.

He's listening.

Am I getting through to him?

"The problem is that it never really did."

"What do you mean?" he asks, furrowing his brows.

"It just never did. I never got the chance to do what I really wanted to do," I say with a shrug. "It's the truth."

My father says nothing in response.

I wait for him, but nothing comes out.

Finally, I look away.

"What am I doing here then?" I ask. "Why did you bring me here?"

My father picks up the leather-bound book from his desk and walks around me.

He is a tall man who hasn't been shrunken by age.

There is no bend in his spine.

His shoulders are broad and imposing just like they've always been.

"I wondered many times why you chose to come back here over and over. I know that you disapproved of this place, and yet every time I called, you came. You just couldn't pull away. You couldn't start your life somewhere else."

My jaw clenches up before I can utter a word.

"I tried. I tried with Alicia."

"Oh, c'mon, you didn't really try," my father

mocks me. "Otherwise, I wouldn't have found out about your plans."

"Why couldn't you just let me go?"

"Because you are my son. And that means you are my property. For life."

I shake my head.

"You are an extension of me. Everything you do is a reflection on me. Don't you know that by now?"

Suddenly, I start to laugh.

It comes from somewhere deep inside of me and it catches me by as much of a surprise as it catches my father.

"If that is really true, then what the fuck does Abbott say about you?" I ask.

My father leaps toward me and wraps his hand around my throat.

I try to breathe in, but nothing comes in.

My airway is completely blocked.

"Now, listen to me, you disrespectful little shit," my father roars into my ear. "You will not speak to me in that manner. I am your father and I am your King."

He lets go of his grasp a little and I start to cough.

Then he yanks his hand away from me and takes a step back.

"Abbott has his demons, but you are a coward.

This is the family you have, and you have turned on it every chance you got. Just like your mother."

With the mention of her, my eyes flare up in anger.

"Oh, yeah, you don't like me talking about her?" he asks, taking notice. "She was just like you. She disapproved of everything. She hated everything about what I was trying to build for us here. For us. For her. Not for me."

I start to laugh again.

I should keep my mouth shut, if I know what's good for me.

I know that.

Of course, I know that.

But I can't.

I've had enough with him.

I've had enough with his games.

I've had enough with everything that this place stands for.

My mother knew the truth about this place and she hated it as much as I do.

If she were here today...I let my thoughts trail off.

I don't know how to finish that.

I don't know what would happen if she were here today.

"You are such a pathetic, egomaniacal fool," I say,

taking a step toward him. "I am not an extension of you. I am nothing like you. The only thing that's a reflection of you is this place. York! The darkness and hate and anger that festers here is because of you. The rage that I feel right now is because of you. So, if you want to know what your legacy will be, look around. You are creating it right now."

My father lunges at me again, but this time I'm ready.

I block his hands from reaching my throat and push him away from me.

Instead of taking it further, he suddenly retreats.

He holds his hands up and takes a step back.

And then he does something completely unexpected.

He begins to laugh.

His laughter is high-pitched and piercing.

It echoes around the room.

"I made this place what I wanted to make this place," he finally says.

"And you think it's full of darkness and hate, but you don't see the beauty in it. The beauty for our family. The prestige. I have presidents and prime ministers of the biggest countries of the world come here and bow down to me and call me King. You think they would do that if we didn't create a place where they could feel safe to be themselves? To enjoy themselves in privacy?"

He shakes his head as he starts to pace around the room. "Your problem is that you don't have vision, son. You could have all of this. You and I both know that Abbott is an idiot. A hot-head. I had so much more hope for you. And that's what I'm most disappointed with."

"Hope for me to do what exactly?"

"To take over for me. To run this place. I really thought that you might come around to seeing things my way. But I guess you are right, I am a fool. You are just like your mother."

"Am I supposed to take that as an insult of some sort?"

CHAPTER 27 - EASTON

WHEN THERE'S NO POINT…

My father looks at me with a perplexed expression on his face.

Is he actually surprised that I would not take a comparison to my mother as an insult, but a compliment?

"My mother was the best thing about you," I finally say. "She was the only good thing about you, and after she died, the only good thing about you died with her."

"Your mother was a bitch and a liar. And you know that as much as I do. And I was happy to get rid of her."

Get rid of her? The words echo in my mind. Get rid of her?

What does he mean by that?

"Yeah, yeah, yeah." My father waves his hand and shrugs his shoulders in response to the shocked look on my face. "Oh, c'mon, you knew. I was getting tired of her and I didn't need her in my life, criticizing me. Like what you are doing now."

"So...you did what exactly?" I whisper.

My hands grow cold as all the blood drains away from them.

A big lump forms in the back of my throat.

I feel my whole body tense up with anger, but I keep it at bay.

I need information. I need him to tell me more.

"You know what I did," my father says cavalierly.

The gravity of his admission doesn't faze him a bit. It's almost as if this is the most obvious thing ever.

"Oh, c'mon, don't look at me like that," he says mockingly. "What? You want me to just come right out with it and say it? Your mother was a problem. She was always a problem. She was always second guessing me, always getting in my way. Whenever I wanted to do something, try something new, her answer was always no. She was too judgmental. Too preachy. Well, one day I'd had enough."

"But mother was sick. She had cancer. She had a long illness."

"You are right about two of those things. yes, she was sick. Yes, it took a long time."

I shake my head. "No, you couldn't have..." I let the words trail off, unable to finish them. Who is this monster I call my father?

"It wasn't that dramatic. It was a poisoning. It was supposed to be faster, but it took a few months."

"A poisoning! And you watched her suffer? All that time?"

"I traveled a lot back then."

I leap toward him and punch him in the mouth.

His head bounces back against the wall of books, but it takes him only a moment to regain his composure.

I don't get the chance to get another blow in because he points the barrel of a gun in my face and presses it to my lips.

"I'm going to blow your fucking head off right now if you don't take a step away from me."

I raise my hands and do as he says.

"You think I'm a moron, son? You think I don't know who the fuck you are? You killed the only friend I ever had."

"You killed my *mother*!" I roar.

I make a move toward him and he shoots the gun.

A bullet whizzes past me and hits the wall.

Suddenly, I don't care anymore.

I'm a dead man as it is and the only thing fueling me now is rage.

Rage at him for killing her.

Rage at myself for not seeing it.

Rage at everything that my life has become.

I lunge at his legs and take him down with one blow.

The gun gets knocked out of his hand.

I search the floor around me for something hard or sharp and wrap my fingers around a metal handle.

When I look up at him again, he is scrambling for the gun.

It's only a few inches away from him.

I try to reach it myself, but there isn't enough time.

It goes off.

The sound is deafening.

But I don't feel a thing.

Am I in shock?

I look down at my torso and arms.

No bullet wounds.

I look down at my father. His body is limp, but still moving.

A little bit.

Struggling for breath.

That's when I spot it.

I'm holding the metal handle in my hand.

The other side of it is a blade, which is covered in blood.

My father's blood.

The knife is ornate and historic looking.

It has sat on top of his desk for ages, mainly used as a letter opener.

It must've fallen onto the floor in our tussle and that's where I grabbed it.

"I didn't think you had it in you, son," my father whispers with blood coming out of his mouth.

Even with his dying breath, he's an asshole.

I wait for him to say anything else, but he doesn't.

He simply closes his eyes and lets go.

I JUMP up to my feet.

I don't have much time.

The guards outside the door, why didn't they come in yet?

Didn't they hear the gun shot? And then I remember.

My father made the doors of his office soundproof for when he doesn't want any prying eyes checking in on what he's doing.

There are also no cameras here.

This is the most private place in the mansion, and that's exactly why I haven't been caught.

Yet.

The clock is ticking.

I have a moment.

I need to seize it.

I have to get away from here.

This is my opportunity.

But how? Everyone knows me.

Everyone knows I've been arrested.

I look around the room for something.

Anything. I need a plan.

If I can't get a plan, then I at least need an idea.

Yes, of course!

I bend down to my father and search his pockets.

It's not there. Why?

Where is it?

I search his desk.

Again, I don't find it.

I search him again.

I'm more careful this time.

I check each pocket individually instead of just patting him down.

And then in the one on his left hip, I find it.

The master key.

The master key opens all rooms and cells and pretty much everything else on the whole island, at least every locked door that I know of.

Whether this will be enough to help me escape remains to be seen.

I look out of the window.

My father's office is on the second floor, and the window swings open easily.

Much to my surprise, it's not locked.

Below me is the eave, which goes around the side of the house along with the wraparound porch.

I lean out of the window to see if anyone is around.

There isn't anyone on this side of the house.

Climbing out onto the eave, I assess the drop.

It's about twelve feet down.

Not too far, but far enough that I could get hurt and twist my ankle.

If I get hurt, that's it.

No, I can't risk anything like that.

Holding onto the edge, I swing my feet over.

I'm just about six feet tall and this would cut the distance I have to travel down in half.

When I land on the ground, I come face-to-face with Mirabelle.

My breath jumps into my throat.

She looks surprised for a moment, but then quickly composes herself.

I don't want to hurt her, but I'm not going to let her stop me.

Without saying a word, I walk past her.

"Easton, wait," she pleads.

"I don't have time for this," I whisper.

"It's Everly."

Hearing her name, I can't help but turn around.

"Where is she? I have to find her."

"She's...in danger. She's with Abbott."

PART SIX

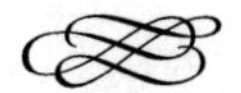

CHAPTER 28 - EVERLY

WHEN HE COMES TO SEE ME...

Easton's words ring in my ears as I walk away from him.

I want to fight the guards, I want to make our moment last longer.

I want to kiss him one more time.

And then one more time above that.

But I can't.

They are here for me and if I fight them, I will make our goodbye that much worse.

I promised him that I won't take my life.

I promised him that I will continue to breathe as long as he does and that promise I intend to keep.

But to marry Abbott?

To make a life here?

No, I cannot do that.

I've known that for a very long time.

But what about that other thing?

The airstrip.

The opportunity to run away.

And not just run away, but to leave this place and rescue him as well?

I want to believe that I can do that, but my fears are getting the best of me.

As I get back to my room, I look at myself in the mirror, and ask myself one question.

"Can you do this, Everly?"

The girl who is looking back at me is scared.

Wide eyes.

Dry mouth.

Filled with memories of the depths of darkness that this place is capable of. And yet, there's that glimmer of hope.

The airstrip is my hope.

Easton told me about it because it's the only way off the island.

But can I do it?

Can I actually escape?

I inhale deeply.

Yes.

I can.

I may be scared.

I may be terrified.

But courage is not the absence of fear.

Courage is to do the thing you were going to do despite of it.

Or perhaps, in spite of it.

All I need is a plan.

I look around the room.

What should I take with me?

The bare essentials, but that would be?

I change into a pair of black yoga pants and a soft, long sleeve V-neck shirt. Also black.

I put on a pair of running shoes.

I put on a baseball hat.

Something to disguise myself, just in case.

I tie my hair up in a ponytail.

What else?

A weapon perhaps?

I search the room for something sharp but find nothing.

If I want to take a knife with me, I'm going to go downstairs and into the kitchen.

If I run into someone there, I can tell them I'm going for a run.

They can't see me taking the knife though.

There's no good explanation for that.

What else? I pace around the room, trying to collect my thoughts. Think strategically.

I look at myself in the mirror again.

I'm ready.

I think I am.

I have to be.

Get it together, Everly.

You can do this.

All you have do is go to the airstrip.

Everything will be fine.

Don't overthink this.

Just go.

With newfound strength and determination, I open the door and run outside, straight into *his* arms.

My whole body goes cold.

It's as if a rush of icy cold air blasts at me.

I take a step back, but he grabs me by my shoulders.

I try to break free and run the opposite direction, but he shoves me back inside my room and locks the door.

"Now, c'mon, c'mon. Don't freak out. I'm not going to hurt you."

His voice is calm.

It is so calm that it comes out like velvet.

He's trying to lure me into a false sense of security.

It's not working.

"What do you want?" I ask.

"I just wanted to come up here. Say hi. Get to know you better."

Abbott's eyes sparkle as the words escape his mouth.

"You don't want to get to know me."

"Oh, I think I do. My brother was obsessed with you. I figured I should at least give you a chance."

Was.

Why did he just use the past tense when talking about Easton?

What does he know that I don't?

Why did I let him lead me back inside?

Why didn't I fight him out in the hallway?

No one knows that we're here.

These thoughts and a million more rush through my mind all at once.

"You see, Everly, I've always had a bit of a problem with jealousy. I hate to admit it, but since you are to be my wife, I don't think we should have any secrets from each other."

I shake my head and move away from him.

But there's nowhere to go.

The room suddenly feels as if it's shrinking around me. It's as if it's physically getting smaller and smaller.

The walls are closing in.

My head starts to spin.

Focus.

You need to focus, I say to myself.

But my body refuses to cooperate.

My heart starts to pound so loudly it feels like it's going to rip through my chest. The gush of rushing blood through my ears makes it impossible to think.

"So, are you going to ignore me now? Is that what you're going to do?" he asks, taking a few steps closer to me.

I retreat until my back collides with the door.

"What are you doing here?" I manage to get out.

"I already told you. I'm jealous. Of my brother, of all people!" His laugh sends shrivers down my spine.

"Why… is that so… unusual?"

"Why? Are you seriously asking me why? Because he's a loser!"

I shake my head.

"You don't agree with me?"

I shake my head again.

"Okay, how about this? Our father gives him everything he could ever want, and he turns his back on it. He doesn't get the power that this place wields. He doesn't get the fact that he could have everything he could ever want here."

"But he can't."

"What?"

"He can't have everything he wants here. All he wanted was to get away from here and live a normal life. All he wanted was to get away from everything that York is and that it represents. And you and his father wouldn't let him. And now, he's sitting in a cell accused of a crime he didn't commit. And you, of all people, are jealous of him? Why the *fuck* are you jealous of him?"

I don't know where these words come from.

They take me by as much of a surprise as they take Abbott.

He stares at me for a moment without saying a word.

CHAPTER 29 - EVERLY

WHEN DARKNESS DESCENDS...

Neither of us speak for what feels like an hour.

He just stares at me and I meet his gaze in return.

It doesn't feel like I have much to lose anymore, so why give him the satisfaction of inciting fear in me.

No, I won't. I'm going to fight.

I'm going to say exactly what's on my mind. And I won't look away.

"So, this is why he loves you," Abbott finally says.

I don't know what he means.

"You are full of surprises, Everly March."

"You don't know the first thing about me."

"I'm starting to realize that."

Another long pause.

He paces around the room and then sits down on the edge of the bed.

He pats the bedspread next to him, inviting me to sit down.

I look at him with the expression on my face that asks, do you think I'm an idiot?

"Whatever, suit yourself," he mumbles under his breath.

"My brother is going to go down for Dagger's murder. You know that, right?"

"No, I don't," I lie. What else is there to say?

"Yes, you do," he says, narrowing his eyes.

"He has a good attorney. He didn't kill him."

"None of that matters."

Now, it's my turn to scrutinize him. Where is all of this confidence coming from? What does he know that I don't?

"You know he didn't do this," I finally say.

"Of course."

"How?"

"Because I did."

Blood drains from my face.

What?

Did I hear that right?

Did Abbott just admit to me that he killed Dagger?

My legs feel weak and suddenly I'm not sure if they are strong enough to hold me up.

"You killed him? Why?"

"Because he's my father's closest advisor. He's his oldest friend. And he never had good things to say about me."

Abbott killed Dagger to protect himself.

I have spent so long looking at everything that has been happening at the house of York through my own lens that it never occurred to me that other people would have their own agendas.

How could I be so self-centered?

Of course, Abbott would have his own power struggle.

Of course, he would find Easton threatening, even though this was the last place on earth that Easton wanted to be.

"You could've had everything. Easton wanted nothing to do with this place. You didn't have to frame him. We would've just left."

"I considered that," Abbott says, lying down on the bed and putting his hands behind his head.

His ability to relax here, in front of me, and feel completely secure that I would never do anything to hurt him, makes me angry.

Rage starts to build somewhere in the pit of my stomach.

"Easton has always said that he wanted nothing from his inheritance or had any interest in a title or anything else. But that wasn't true, was it?"

"Of course, it was."

"He asked father to marry you."

"So what?"

"So what? That's all our father ever wanted. A line. A legacy. All of that bullshit. Why the fuck do you think he gets married every two years and has all of those goddamn kids with his new wives?"

"If that's what he wanted, then why didn't you give it to him?"

He sits up on the bed.

"I never met anyone good. Besides, I thought I would have more time. I thought that Easton would go away. Or at least, would do something to make him mad enough to send him away for good. I didn't realize that he would agree to marry you and start his life here as a proper prince of York."

I shake my head.

Tears of anger and rage are starting to well up deep within me.

He framed Easton for no reason at all.

He could've had everything he wanted, and we could've had everything we wanted.

And now...now, everything is all fucked up.

"We didn't want to do any of that. We could've left. Easton just didn't think he had a choice. Your father was so excited..." I start tripping over my words as I speak.

He walks over to me and wraps his arms around me.

My body shudders and I try to break free, but he holds me tightly.

"Shhhh, it's going to be alright," he says softly.

My skin starts to crawl.

What is he doing?

Why is he holding me like this?

What is this tenderness and why is it making me feel sick to my stomach?

"Why did you do that?" I ask, looking up at him. "You didn't have to. We would've left. You could've had everything. All he wanted was me."

Abbott looks deep into my eyes.

At first, his gaze is soft. Kind, even.

But then, within a moment, it turns to ice.

I try to pull away from him, but he slams me into the wall.

My head collides with it hard and I start to see stars in my peripheral vision.

"Don't you see?" he asks with a loud thunderous laugh. "You just answered your own question."

I don't respond, so he slams me into the wall again.

"Easton wants you. And I can't let him have you."

"Why?" I whisper.

"Because you're going to be mine."

He grabs me by my hair and drags me to the bed.

He flips me over and tries to pull down my pants.

But before he succeeds, I turn over and knee him in the groin.

Hard.

As hard as I can.

He curses at me and topples over.

I run over to the dresser and grab the glass vase with both hands.

Without giving him another opportunity to attack me, I smash it over his head.

Suddenly, blood is everywhere.

Abbott lies on his back, barely moving.

Whimpering.

I kneel down next to him, trying to collect my thoughts.

What do I do now?

Finish him off or just make a run for it.

If he isn't as hurt as he seems, then he'll catch up with me.

And then, I might not have another chance.

But still, taking a life that's lying helplessly in front of me, seems impossible.

I am not a cold-blooded murderer after all.

Even though he is.

"Fuck you," Abbott whispers.

The tone of his voice makes my blood turn to ice and I grab a large piece of broken glass from the floor.

When he moves, I see that he is holding a gun with his left hand and I fall to the floor and lodge the glass in his throat.

Blood bubbles out of his mouth and his body grows limp.

His hand relaxes, and the gun falls to the floor.

But I no longer trust my eyes.

I reach for his hand and try to find a pulse.

I don't let out a sigh of relief until I am certain that he no longer has one.

CHAPTER 30 - EVERLY

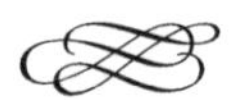

WHEN I MAKE A RUN FOR IT...

After I am certain that Abbott is dead, I run into the closet and change out of my blood-stained clothes.

I want to take a shower, but I don't have time.

I need to get away from here before anyone knows what happened.

My only chance now is to make it to that airstrip.

I close the door gently behind me and walk down the hallway.

My heart is beating out of my chest, but I don't let it faze me.

I have a plastic smile on my face.

I curl my lips a little bit and try not to look too overeager.

I'm just going on a walk. I'm not doing anything suspicious.

"Hey! Everly!" Savannah calls my name.

I stop in my tracks, but don't dare turn around.

"Want to go swimming?" Teal asks.

I don't, no.

But thanks for asking, I want to say.

Of course, I don't.

"No, not right now," I say a little bit too quickly. "I gotta go."

"Where are you going?" one of them asks.

They aren't prying.

They're genuinely interested.

Act like everything's fine.

"I'm just going on a walk," I say and take a few steps back toward the door.

The girls are congregating in the kitchen, and I hope that they stay there.

"Oh, that can wait!" Savannah announces. "Come here. Come over."

I debate as to what I should do.

I can stay, but then I will lose time.

If I leave too quickly, then they might start to suspect something.

Please, please, please.

I plead for nothing in particular.

No, that's not true.

I plead for the universe to let me pass.

I plead for one goddamn break.

Peeking out from behind the doorway, I can feel them waiting for me.

I rub my hand on the back of my neck.

Perhaps, I should go there.

Perhaps, I need to make an appearance to buy myself some time.

Pulling my palm away from my neck, I see blood.

It's coming from right below my hair line.

It doesn't really hurt when I touch it, but I can feel the wet liquid and I see the red blood.

"I'm sorry, I really can't!" I yell and disappear behind the front door.

As soon as the door slams shut, I begin to run.

I no longer care about trying to stay in the shadows.

I'm wearing workout pants and sneakers.

I could be out on a run.

I have an excuse; what I don't have is time.

I need to get to the airstrip as fast as possible.

If the girls weren't alerted by my odd behavior, I'm sure that the guards were. Or whoever was watching the monitors.

I run.

I run with my feet kicking high and I run until my chest starts to ache.

When I get a stitch in my side, I take a deep breath and pick up the pace.

I run when I think that I can't run anymore. And I run when tears start to run down my face.

There's something about pushing your body to its limit that makes you totally emotionally fragile.

It's as if my body is about to break in two, but before it does, my mind does.

I don't know how I'm going to convince this stranger to trust me.

I don't know what getting to the airstrip is going to do for me.

All I know is that I don't have much time.

The universe doesn't give you that many chances, and I seem to have wasted all of mine.

The airstrip appears just a few feet after the pathway leading into the jungle disappears. I follow it to the end of the bend and then I keep going.

I wish I had a machete to clear some of the brush, or to protect myself.

Either way, a machete would definitely make me feel a lot better about this whole situation.

The airstrip isn't anything like I've seen before.

It's small, big enough for one plane to take off and land, and basically looks like a large driveway which has been somewhat cleared of grass.

But only somewhat.

The jungle surrounds it on both sides.

And I'm no aviation expert, but I've seen a movie or two about smuggling drugs from Columbia.

And this airstrip looks barely long enough for a small plane to take off from.

Nevertheless, I am certain that I'm in the right place.

I make my way along the brush toward what looks like a bus stop in the middle of nowhere.

And not any fancy city bus stop with plastic windows and a proper roof.

No, this one has a strip of tin across four pieces of plywood and two plastic chairs.

Is that where people are supposed to wait for their flights? I wonder.

Then suddenly, I see him.

Or rather them.

A big guy with dark hair and large sweat stains underneath his armpits.

That has to be Daniel.

But what about the skinny blonde one wearing the same uniform?

Who the hell is that?

Another security guard, I'm sure.

But what the hell am I supposed to do with him?

CHAPTER 31 - EVERLY

WHEN I MAKE A RUN FOR IT...

I retreat a little bit into the bushes to try to figure out what to do next.

I can't just come up to them.

What would I say?

I hadn't planned this through enough.

And unfortunately, Easton hadn't mentioned this possibility.

And what if he did? My mind wanders.

What would've been different then?

Nothing. Not really. Complications are always a possibility, right?

This is just one of those things.

Okay, Everly. Focus.

Stop letting your mind wander.

Stop meandering.

For all I know, they could already be looking for you. They could've found Abbott's body and they could have the guards after you. You need to make a decision.

I look around and assess the situation as best as I can. Daniel and the skinny guy are sitting on two plastic chairs in what looks to be a movable mobile office.

It looks like one of those sheds they sell outside of Home Depots back home.

It has a few windows to allow a breeze through and some audio-visual equipment. There is a large desk that spans from one side of the shed to another with a few laptops and other controls.

Given what I know about York, I would think that this place would be a little better equipped.

Maybe a real office for the guards. Or some sort of security checkpoint. But perhaps, that's why Easton sent me here.

Perhaps, no one really knows about this place or how poorly it is guarded. Or maybe it's not really meant to be known.

Did Easton say this was a little private airport? This is definitely not the place that the king or any royals would land in.

It's also unlikely that this is the place that they

would accept important visitors to the island, like other heads of state.

I'm not certain of much, but I'm certain about that.

So, what is this place?

Perhaps, it's what it looks like it is.

A tiny private airport for some non-important locals to come and go off the island. Just as the thought goes through my mind, I see a small plane start to descend.

I hide further into the bushes and watch as it lands and makes its way down the strip. The guards wait for the pilot to come out before helping him unload the cargo.

So, that's what this place is, I say to myself.

This must be where the freight comes into. Like the freight elevator in a fancy condo building, this is where all the supplies for York come in.

I watch and wait as the plane gets unpacked.

Luckily, the pilot didn't come in with much, just a few boxes, which he wheels away on dollies.

Daniel and the skinny guy help him load them and then return to their post and their sandwiches.

But then, the pilot has trouble managing the dolly.

The boxes are just a bit too big and unwieldy.

The skinny guy offers to help and they disappear down the path away from the strip.

I watch as Daniel returns to his post and his sandwich, unable to believe my luck.

Did this just really happen?

Do I really have him alone?

I still have no idea what I'm going to say to him, but I know that this is my chance. I walk up to the booth and knock on the side of it.

When he looks up at me, it's clear that I'm the last person he's expecting to see.

"Hi, I'm sorry to bother you..." I start to say.

"You are...wait, aren't you?" he asks, taking a particularly large bite and then choking on it a little.

I don't know who he thinks I am but I wait for him to wash it down with the soda before continuing.

"Aren't you Everly?"

"Yes, I am. You know who I am?"

"Everyone knows who you are."

"Okay, great. Listen, I need your help."

I decide against mincing words and to come straight out and ask him.

There's no other way to ask him to help me without actually asking him to help me.

So, why make things complicated?

He stares at me and waits for me to continue.

"I need you to fly me off this island. Easton told me that you could do this for me. For him."

"No, no, no..." he starts to say.

"Daniel, please. They arrested him. He's awaiting trial for something he didn't do and they're going to frame him. Then they're going to make me marry Abbott."

The expression on his face softens for a moment.

"I'm sorry about that, but if I help you escape, they will find out who did it. I have a family to think of."

"But you owe Easton. He helped you and now you have to help me."

"Easton did a great thing for me," Daniel says after a moment. "I know that. But...I can't do this. They will know. They will find out."

I take his hands into mine. "You don't have to come back here. Easton told me that your family lives off the island. If you fly me off this island, I will pay you. Enough for you and your family to start your life somewhere else, far away from here. Don't you want that?"

"They'll find us."

"We will get you new identities," I say. "He will

pay you two-hundred thousand dollars. But only after you help me. Daniel, please."

I look into his eyes.

I can see him considering this.

There's a chance.

I continue to talk.

I continue to lay out the plans that Easton had proposed to me.

I continue because I have to convince him.

This is my only chance.

As I talk, I continue to hold his hands in mine and he doesn't push me away.

The hardened, distant look on his face is turning into something else.

I don't know anything about him, but I have a feeling that his job here isn't exactly voluntary.

He isn't a prisoner like I am, but he's not far from it.

He works here because he doesn't have another option...until now.

"This is your chance at a new life, Daniel. Yours and your family's chance to begin anew. Please, you have to help me."

Daniel takes a deep breath and gives me a small nod.

CHAPTER 32 - EVERLY

WHEN THERE'S A COMPLICATION...

Yes?

Is that a yes?

I stare at him in disbelief.

"Okay, let's go," I say quickly, not wanting to give him the chance to change his mind.

He gives me a wink.

A part of me can't believe that it was this easy to convince him, but I don't push my luck.

He said yes and that's all that's important.

That's all that matters.

There is of course one complication.

For some reason, it hadn't occurred to me until this moment.

But suddenly, it is ridiculously obvious.

"How do we get off this island?" I ask.

"We have to take his plane," Daniel says, walking away from me.

I look up and down the tarmac in search of another option.

Unfortunately, there are no other planes in sight.

"But then they'll know right away," I say.

The pilot will come back and see that his plane is missing along with the security guard.

He gives me a shrug.

"Do you have another idea?"

I don't.

Not at all.

For some reason, I thought that he maybe had another plane to use.

Maybe it would be stashed away somewhere in the jungle, just for this kind of emergency.

But that would be ridiculous.

"The only way off this island is to take his plane. But if we do, then they'll know what we did right away. They will send out a search party. We will not have much time to get away."

The gravity of his voice sends shivers through my body.

He is sweating profusely and his speech is rushed, and I know that this decision to help me will impact him for the rest of his life.

"You cannot bullshit me, Everly. Please don't lie to me. If I help you, you have to help me and my family start a new life with new identities. The king will never stop looking for me for doing this."

I nod and promise that I will.

"I will do everything in my power to help you. I promise. And with the money that Easton told me about, you can start a new life far away from here."

He takes a deep breath and then heads toward the plane.

"Are you coming?"

It takes me a moment to realize that we are actually leaving right this minute.

I watch as Daniel labors and huffs climbing into the pilot seat and I climb into the seat next to him.

Technically, this is also the pilot's seat since all I see in front of me are buttons and the control yoke for actually flying the plane.

"Don't we need the key?" I ask.

I've never sat inside of a plane like this and I have no idea what anything is called, let alone what any of the buttons do.

"He left it inside," Daniel says, pointing to the keys in the ignition.

I nod and let out a big sigh of relief.

Daniel starts to press on various buttons to get

the plane moving and as he does this, I feel the tension in my shoulders start to relax.

It's one of those things you don't even notice is tense until one moment when it's not anymore and suddenly an unfamiliar feeling of relaxation starts to sweep through your body.

This is it.

This is actually happening, I say to myself.

I'm going to get off this God forsaken island for good.

The engine catches and the plane starts to move.

I look out of the window at the horizon. I'm going home. I'm almost there. A big gulp starts to form in the back of my throat.

It's going to be okay.

After everything I've been through, it's actually going to be okay.

"Get the fuck out of the plane!" His voice is distant and far away, but he repeats himself again.

The plane starts to slow down and I shake my head.

The other guard is back and he's standing on Daniel's side of the plane, pointing a gun at him.

"No, we have to keep going," I say, pressing on the yoke in front of me.

I don't know how to fly but I can't let him stop us now.

We are too close.

"I've got a gun and I'm not afraid to use it!" the other guard yells, shooting a round in the air.

"Daniel, please," I plead.

"He's going to shoot us!" he screams.

"No, he won't!" I say, even though I have no idea if that's true or not.

But before he decides either way, suddenly the other guard is tossed onto the ground.

Daniel leans over to look through his window, blocking my view entirely.

I stand up in my seat and that's when I finally see him.

It's Easton.

And he is on top of the guard, punching him in his face. I open the door and jump out of the plane.

Easton knocked the gun out of the guard's hand, but it hasn't landed far away from him.

I pick it up and point it at him.

When he swings at Easton, I yell for him to stop.

Seeing me with it, he finally gives up the fight.

Easton gives me a smile.

"You got any rope back there?" he yells.

Daniel fishes around in the back and emerges with some rope.

He helps Easton tie up the guard to the nearest palm tree as I stand with my gun pointed at him.

When the guard is finally secure, Easton walks over and takes the gun out of my hand.

I let go and wrap my arms around him.

"What are you doing here? How the hell did you get away?" I feel his shoulders and arms just to make sure that I am not dreaming.

"It's a long story," he whispers. "Are you ready to get out of here?"

I nod.

"Okay, good, because we don't have much time." He presses his lips onto mine and gives me a big warm kiss with a bit of tongue.

"I missed you, Everly. Oh, how I've missed you." He kisses me again.

"Okay, okay, let's go. You two are the most wanted people here. You have to get as far away from here as possible. And fast."

Her voice comes as a surprise.

Can it really be her?

"Mirabelle?" I ask.

PART SEVEN

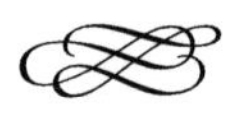

CHAPTER 33 - EVERLY

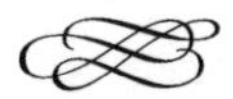

WHEN I SEE THE BLUE...

Mirabelle and I cram into the back of the plane with Daniel and Easton in the front. This time, I do not feel my shoulders relax until we lift off the ground and clear the trees.

In fact, I don't fully relax until we are over the water. The water below is the color of turquoise, the kind of water that dreams are made of.

Not so long ago, I, too, dreamed of escaping to a Caribbean island and leaving the real world behind.

And now, I can't wait to get back to it.

"I never thought that I would ever leave York," Mirabelle says as we fly into the horizon.

The water below us turns from turquoise to dark blue and becomes as flat as glass.

"I never knew you wanted to," I say. "I thought

that you were...the King's loyal subject. Well, you know what I mean."

The words 'loyal subject' come out strange and feel awkward in my mouth.

"I had to be what I had to be. But no, I don't think you could say I was ever loyal." She gives me a wink and a smile.

"Is that why you were helping me all of that time?" I ask.

"I wish I could say yes, but that would be a lie. I was helping you because I felt sorry for you. And over the years I have helped many girls with advice and guidance about how to make it here, if they were willing to accept it. But to be honest, I never thought you would ever get off this island. No one else ever has."

There are of course other girls who have left this island before.

The ones who have been sold off to the highest bidder.

But both she and I know that their fates are nothing to be jealous of.

Mirabelle and I don't speak for a few minutes.

I look out of the window and watch as pelicans gracefully fly below us and land on the water.

"So, how did you end up here?" I ask.

"It's all ancient history," she says after a moment.

I nod. Despite how much I want to know more about her, her real self, this is not the right time. We are flying away from York and away from the darkness that it stands for. So, why bring it with us? Whatever happened there is in the past and will hopefully remain there.

Despite my best intentions, however, my mind continues to wander.

My thoughts keep swirling back to all those unanswered questions that remain there.

What about those other girls?

What about Savannah and Teal and the others at the house?

And what about all those others in the dungeons?

What will become of them?

"The king will never stop looking for you," I say. "You know that, right?"

Mirabelle doesn't turn her eyes away from the window.

Suddenly, a little smile forms in the corner of her lips.

"The king is dead."

* * *

Her words ring in my ears during the rest of the flight.

I ask her what happened and she glosses over thc details.

He requested to see Easton in his private chambers.

He attacked him.

Easton killed him.

There is more to it than that, but that's all she knows. But the details are almost inconsequential to me right now.

Dead.

The king is dead.

An unfamiliar giddy feeling forms in the pit of my stomach and it quickly makes its way up my body.

I'm actually physically happy to hear this news.

With the king dead and Abbott dead, that leaves...Easton to carry on the darkness of York.

But there's no way he would do that.

I tell Mirabelle about Abbott and she gives me a smile.

"I was hoping that's what happened. That man had it coming for a very long time."

"So, what's going to happen now?" I ask. "To York?"

Mirabelle inhales deeply and lets her shoulders straighten out into a long shrug. She looks away from me. This isn't good.

"What? I thought that if the king and the prince are dead then…it would be over."

Mirabelle shakes her head.

"You may be right, but…"

Her words trail off.

"What?"

"I'm not sure. I mean, yes, they are both gone so that's something. Easton is here, and he is the next in line for the throne. But that doesn't mean that there aren't others who want York to continue."

I fly for a few more minutes in silence.

Whatever glee I felt only a short time ago is suddenly gone.

But perhaps I should just be happy that it's all over.

For me, anyway. I am safe. Easton is safe.

THAT WAS NEVER SUPPOSED to happen, and yet here we are, flying away from that awful dark place into the light.

But no matter how much I try to convince myself

that this is enough, my thoughts keep swirling back to Savannah. And Catalina.

And all the other women who are left back there.

Waiting.

In danger of being hurt.

"Why are you two so quiet back there? What's wrong?" Easton turns to us.

His voice is elevated, but I can hear him perfectly fine through the headphones.

"I was just thinking about the rest of the women. What's going to happen to them now?"

Easton turns in his seat to face me. I look up at him. His eyes are twinkling. There's a smile on his face.

"What?" I ask. "What is it?" I have to know. I can't wait any longer.

"York is over."

CHAPTER 34 - EASTON

WHEN IT'S REALLY OVER…

I wanted to wait to tell Everly everything when we were in private.

Or rather when we weren't on a plane with the wind howling outside. I wanted to tell her everything when I could wrap my arms around her and bury my hands in her hair.

But at the same time, I also wanted her to know this as soon as possible.

"York is over," I say again and wait for her expression to change from confused to something resembling excitement.

Unfortunately, she doesn't.

She furrows her eyebrows and looks even more lost.

"What do you mean?" she asks into her headset.

I dig through my bag for the external hard drive.

It's a small solid box, about the size of my smartphone.

"What is that?"

"This is proof. Of everything that has been going on on that island. Proof of everything that everyone has done."

She shakes her head in disbelief.

I go on to explain that everything there has been recorded.

Even things that were really not in the best interest of being recorded, like the abuse that happened in the dungeons, were recorded and kept just in case.

"My father made lots of promises to lots of powerful men that he will keep their secrets. But he made the recordings anyway, just in case he ever needed their help. As blackmail. Well, now, he's dead. And I never made any such promises, and I would never keep those kinds of secrets."

She stares at me, dumbfounded.

I know she can hear me.

I'm just not sure if she is fully processing everything I'm saying.

"So, what's going to happen now?" she asks. "Are you going to blackmail them?"

"Who?"

"All of the men in the videos?"

"Hell no," I say. The thought had never even crossed my mind. How is she still not getting this?

"After we pick up Daniel's family, we are headed straight to Washington DC. I know of an attorney I can trust and he will put me in contact with the right people in government to handle this situation. This is top secret information and if we play our cards right, we will ruin many people's lives."

She gives me a wide smile. It goes from ear to ear and lights up her whole face.

People are going to pay for what they have done here.

Charges will be filed.

And the media will be notified.

Everyone who came here and did bad things here will have their name lit up brightly.

My chest tightens up at the audacity of what I am about to do. It's going to be hard. I myself will likely be questioned and interrogated and investigated.

But I am prepared to tell them the truth about everything. I want my father's name to be tarnished forever.

I want him to be synonymous with all of those

other monsters throughout the world that caused so much suffering.

Hitler. Stalin. Pol Pot. Kim Jong-Un.

"What if it doesn't work?" Everly asks after a moment.

There's a look of concern on her face.

"It has to," I say.

"But whatever is on those recordings...those men do not want that out."

"Yes, I know that. And they will do anything to stop us."

She shakes her head.

What was just a moment of excitement and opportunity suddenly morphs into something else.

I know why she's worried. It's not every day that you have the chance to ruin the lives of five heads of state, at least ten of their second and third in command and countless other important figures.

My father made connections with many powerful men, including five billionaires from Forbes Magazine's Richest People list, and generals, and admirals from the armed services.

Obviously, I haven't seen all the recordings - that's one of the things we'll be doing in DC.

But I know who is on there because I've seen the people in real life.

My father couldn't resist the opportunity to wine and dine them during their stays here.

"Our only advantage is that no one knows anything about what happened there yet," I say, reaching back and taking her hand in mine. "No one knows that my father and Abbott are dead. I'm not sure anyone on the island knows much of anything yet. And that's why we have to do this fast."

She doesn't say much after that.

Daniel calls his wife from the air and tells her to meet us at the airstrip.

She sounds surprised, but not all that shocked.

I am certain that he had been preparing her and the kids for this eventuality and they meet us when we land.

They only have two suitcases with them, with their barest possessions.

The little girl is holding their cat.

"I couldn't make her leave the cat," his wife says, wrapping her arms tightly around him. "I said it would be your decision."

The little girl looks up at Daniel with a mixture of tears and hope in her eyes. But Daniel shakes his head.

He kneels down to her and puts his hand on the back of her head.

"We can't take him, honey. We don't know where we are going," he says, his voice cracking from his heartbreak.

Tapping on his shoulder, I lean over and whisper into his ear. "Let her bring the cat. It's a member of your family. I don't want you to leave anyone behind."

"But what about staying in hotels? Not pet-friendly apartments? It will be a… complication."

The little girl bursts into tears and clutches the cat even tighter.

"Let me worry about that," I say. "We aren't leaving anyone behind."

When Daniel's family climbs into the back of the plane, the little girl squeezes in right next to Everly.

The last thing I see as we pull away from the ground is Everly petting the cat's head as it snuggles up to her.

CHAPTER 35 - EVERLY

WHEN WE WAIT...

We spend almost two weeks in Washington DC, hiding out before the raid.

Easton meets with his attorney and that meeting is quickly followed by about a hundred more. They talk for hours each day to strategize and make plans.

I don't see him for days, but we text and talk on the phone during practically every free minute that he has.

The phones we use are special phones, provided by the FBI, to make sure that they are not intercepted and our conversations are kept private.

Well, I doubt that they are entirely private.

The phones are provided by the FBI and I

wouldn't be surprised if the conversations are recorded as well.

But I don't care.

Before we got to DC, Easton and I made a pact.

A promise to each other.

We would tell them the truth. In order to bring York to justice, we cannot have any secrets.

Yes, that includes the fact that he killed his father. And yes, that includes the fact that I killed Abbott.

Neither crimes have been discussed in much detail yet with any of the attorneys, or prosecutors and special agents handling the situation, but it's not something we are going to hide.

"I want everything that happened in York to be public," Easton said to me when we made this promise to each other. "And in order for that to happen, we can't hide anything from them."

I agree with him.

Of course, I do.

Yet, there's still a part of me that has its doubts.

I mean, what if they don't believe us?

What if they prosecute us for killing them, even though it was in self-defense?

There are thousands of innocent people sitting

in prisons all over America, what's to say we won't be two more?

But Easton's confidence is steadfast and unwavering.

He refuses to believe that anymore badness will come our way.

And he is laser-focused on bringing York and everyone who participated in its injustices to justice.

While Easton goes over all the details over and over again, I wait in the safe house that the FBI has placed me into.

In movies, safe houses always look small and dark and dirty.

But this two-bedroom apartment is nothing like that.

It's actually quite nice. I've only been to DC on a seventh grade school field trip, so I have no idea where in the city we are exactly, but I do have a nice view of a large park where kids play in the afternoons.

There are two agents stationed to stay with me in the apartment, on rotation.

They don't talk much, but they laugh when I watch reruns of Fraser, Friends, and the Office on Netflix and I like that.

I should probably watch something more

contemporary, but I don't have the energy to engage with anything new.

The old shows serve as background noise.

I've seen them numerous times and I can just have them on without really engaging with the subject matter in any serious way that requires attention.

The day that it all goes down is like any other.

The trees outside my window are naked and sway only a little bit when the wind swirls around them.

I turn up the episode of Friends in which Winona Ryder plays Jennifer Aniston's sorority sister just to drown my own thoughts as I stare out of the window.

The show and the laugh track aren't enough though.

My thoughts keep tumbling through without my consent.

I look at the time.

A second passes and the raid begins.

There are thirty-seven men in the United States who are being served arrest warrants at this exact moment.

They are being woken up in their beds in penthouses and lavish estates. It's the middle of the night because some of the men are on the west coast.

Those who are not located in the United States, are being arrested in their homes abroad by other jurisdictions.

All of the raids are coordinated and arranged to occur at precisely the same moment so that everyone is surprised at exactly the same time.

As soon as all the men are taken into custody, they will hold a joint press conference with everyone involved in orchestrating the raids.

"Let's watch," the agent says, flipping to the news.

I listen to the commercial and keep looking out of the window.

A group text comes in from Easton to me, Mirabelle, and Daniel.

It's over. Everything went according to plan.

I let out a small sigh of relief.

I can't fully relax quite yet though.

I wait for the news.

I hear the announcer apologize for interrupting their scheduled programming with breaking news and the story begins to unfold.

They have footage of what happened only a few hours ago on York. I see women being escorted from the property and onto planes by agents.

There are bright lights and most of them have tears.

In one clip, I recognize the outlines of their silhouettes. It's Savannah and Teal.

But the others I don't.

They have blankets around them and they huddle next to each other for safety.

As the tape continues to roll, I see that some are being taken out on gurneys.

The news anchor talks, reading from a script.

The words come in and out of my mind and make me dizzy.

"Dungeon."

"Sex trafficking."

"Kept as slaves."

"Competition to marry."

"Many wives."

"Fathered a lot of children."

Each word brings about a different memory until I can't bear to listen to it anymore.

I sit down and bury my head in my hands.

The agent turns off the television and apologizes.

The rest of the day is a blur, just like the one after, and the one after that. Different people with badges and important sounding jobs come to talk to me.

Some are pleasant while others are rude. Some raise their voices and others try to be my friends.

But they all have the same agenda. They interrogate me. They ask me the same questions over and over again.

They ask about everything and anything about my stay in York. Despite how tired and annoyed I get, I answer all of their questions.

I don't generalize, and I don't lie.

I don't hide a thing.

I have a lawyer with me, who tells me to be quiet, but I don't listen to him.

Easton and I made a pact.

To expose the truth about York, we are going to tell the truth about everything.

And then, one day, it's finally over.

PART EIGHT

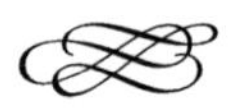

CHAPTER 36 - EVERLY

MONTHS LATER...

After all that time in the sun, the nip of the cold feels refreshing on the tip of my nose. My cheeks are burning red and the tips of my fingers are numb. I am out of breath, scrambling up to the top of the hill, even though Easton has carried up both his sled and mine to make things easier.

"Aren't there those sledding places where you stand on the conveyer belt and they drag you up?" I ask, pausing in the middle of the hill to catch my breath.

"Yes, there are," Easton says with a laugh. "But then we wouldn't have all of this."

I turn around and look down into the valley.

The hill is covered in virgin snow that sparkles in the sunlight.

The trees at the top and around the periphery stand proud and tall.

Their long needles are covered in snow, creating a cushion of feathers. I slip and break my fall with my hands.

"Are you okay?" Easton asks.

I nod and start to laugh.

The snow makes a crinkling sound under my body as I struggle to get up.

I glance at my gloves, which are covered in perfect six-sided snowflakes.

The bright blue sky above us, each one sparkles with vibrant hues.

Finally, I wobble up the hill and fall into his arms.

He takes my head into his hands and kisses me on the mouth.

His lips are cold, but his mouth is warm, and I know that I am home.

"You really want to give up all of this for a conveyer belt and the crowds?" Easton asks when he pulls away from me and turns me down toward the empty valley.

There isn't another human soul in sight.

What there is instead is an eagle flying high

above us and the crinkling of snow below our footsteps.

"Never," I say and lay my head on his shoulder.

We stand here for a few minutes, in total silence.

The eagle flies in circles, going nowhere in particular. Nature shows will have us believe that all animals are always locked in an epic struggle for life or death. That's how they create drama and excitement.

But in reality, most of the time, animals, and birds, and other living things do what all of us living things do when we don't have anything better to do.

Live life by enjoying the little moments.

"I love you," Easton whispers.

His words are barely audible and though I know they are directed at me, he is saying them more to the universe than anything else.

"I love you, too," I whisper. "Now, let's race!"

I grab my sled from him and sit down.

Both sleds are old-fashioned wooden types with metal runners and a rope you use to control it.

I grew up using plastic saucers and I've never seen ones like these except in catalogs and Christmas movies, but are the only ones they had back at the cabin.

"Now or never!" I say, urging him to sit down.

"We have to start at the same time for this to be a proper race!"

Easton gets on his sled and we count down. On three, we both push off.

Well, sort of.

I had miscalculated the start and have to push myself off with my feet to just get moving.

I look down the hill and Easton is flying away from me.

Shit. Shit. Shit.

I grab onto the rope tightly and scrunch my body as small as it can go.

The wind is whizzing past me, making my whole body shudder from the pins and needles.

I close my eyes for a second and when I open them, I sled past him.

How's that even possible?

He picks up some speed but not enough to win.

At the bottom of the hill, I jump from my sled and wrestle him to the ground.

"You let me win!" I squeal. "You can't let me win!"

"Why not?" he asks innocently.

"Because... it's not fair."

"Well, it was a false start then," he says, flipping me over on my back and pinning me to the ground.

"Yeah, on my end. I couldn't get the damn thing to move," I say.

He lays on top of me, pressing his body into mine.

Our mouths touch and our tongues intertwine. He pulls off his gloves and runs his fingers down my jaw.

He pulls down my scarf just a bit, exposing my neck to the cold, but then quickly covers it up with his warm soft fingers.

Then he kisses me again.

And again.

And again.

CHAPTER 37 - EVERLY

COMING HOME...

This is our second day in Vermont and even though it has only been a few months,

York feels like a lifetime ago.

The raid went as well as could be expected and everyone has been arrested.

Due to the plethora of evidence, the majority of men have pled guilty in exchange for shorter sentences, but none are less than twenty years in maximum security prisons.

All of the women have been freed. Those who wanted them were given new identities.

Since the men were in such positions of power with a lot of wealth and means, all the victims are pursuing civil lawsuits against them and they will likely result in multi-million-dollar verdicts.

It won't do much in changing the past but it will do a lot of damage to the perpetrators, which is all you can ask for.

I'm one of the victims involved in the civil lawsuits.

Due to the tapes, the investigators were able to identify the men who were involved in violating me in the dungeons.

Luckily (for legal purposes) they were all Americans, so the lawsuits were easy to bring about.

Since they all pled guilty, the amount that I'm going to receive is not clear, but it will be enough to set me up for life.

I don't want the money, but I want them to pay.

I am not decided yet, but I am thinking of starting a foundation to help women who have been trafficked, and whatever money I do receive will likely go there to help others.

The investigators have cleared both Easton and me of any wrongdoing and as soon as we were free to leave the city, we headed straight to Vermont.

I'm not sure which one of us suggested it exactly except that we both wanted to go somewhere cold with a lot of nature.

We haven't been alone together, really alone, ever, and this was the perfect spot.

"You think we'll ever see Daniel and Mirabelle again?" I ask as we walk back to our cabin after sledding.

It's about a mile walk down a winding path, which has recently been cleared.

We are dragging our sleds through the snow and they make a loud swishing sound somewhere under our footsteps.

"We should give them some space first, but then if you want, I can try to find out their new names and where they live."

"Eh," I say, shrugging.

All I know is that they both decided to start their lives over again in the Sun Belt.

Mirabelle in Arizona and Daniel in New Mexico.

Or is it the other way around?

In any case, I'm glad that they are okay, but I don't really have any interest in reaching out to them anytime soon.

The only reason we know each other is because of this horrible thing we've all been through in York.

And that makes for a dubious foundation for a friendship.

We finally walk up to our snow-covered cabin.

It's a remodeled, 1940s, knotty pine cabin, with a loft upstairs.

From the entrance, it doesn't look like much.

Just quaint, and cute, and charming.

Snow piled on top of the roof, and windows with shutters looking out onto the road. But the beauty of the place is from the inside. Inside, the cabin has a fifteen-foot ceiling and glass windows going up to the top of it.

After stomping our feet from the snow, we head inside and Easton starts a fire in the large fireplace.

I plop down on the expansive couch and recline the seat.

Out in the distance, I watch as the winds circle around the peaks of the mountains.

A large open valley of white spans before us and three deer prance across the snow. When the fire starts raging in front of us and makes it warm enough for me to pull off my sweater, Easton sits down next to me.

"Your feet are freezing," he says as I tuck them under him.

"Well, it's twenty degrees outside."

He takes off my socks and starts to rub them with his warm, strong hands.

Each time he adds pressure to me, my whole body relaxes more and more.

Then something occurs to me.

"Tomorrow is Christmas and I haven't even gotten you anything."

"I haven't gotten you anything either," he says. "I actually completely forgot about Christmas."

"Me, too," I confess. "But I guess it's okay. I mean, we've been through a lot, right?"

He nods.

"Besides, I sort of think that this is enough."

I nod.

This is more than enough. I lean over and kiss him. Never in a million years did I think that we would be here. I mean, I wished it. I prayed for it. I hoped for it. But looking back, the idea that Easton and I could actually end up together escaped me. I mean, how? How did we end up here? How was this even possible?

He gives me a small smile. It's a bit crooked on the left side, a fact that I just noticed since we've been here. In this cabin, away from the stress of everything that we've been through during our time together, I suddenly notice a lot more things about him that I hadn't before. Like the way he rubs the knuckles on his left hand with his right when he has something exciting to tell me. Or the way he broadens his shoulders when he relaxes his body into mine. And even just the way every muscle in his face relaxes when we are both sitting on the couch and watching the fire flicker in the fireplace.

"I want to stay here forever," I say.

"I do, too."

He lifts up my chin to his and holds it there for a moment.

He looks deep into my eyes and it's almost as if this is his first time looking at me.

Then he lowers his head and pulls the sleeve of my t-shirt off my shoulder. Goose bumps run up my arms and make the small hairs on them stand up from excitement.

I curl my toes and reach my mouth toward his.

But he presses his finger to my lips and stops me.

"What are you doing?" I mumble.

Instead of answering, he pulls down my sleeve even further and kisses my collarbone.

Then he pulls down the strap of my bra and kisses the skin just below my neck.

I tilt my head back, losing myself in the moment.

CHAPTER 38 - EVERLY

AS THE SNOW FALLS...

After caressing my neck with his lips, Easton pulls off my shirt and unclasps my bra.

My breasts fall into his open mouth and he gently pushes my body back against the couch.

He climbs on top of me and presses his lips onto my mouth.

There he finds my tongue and entertains his with mine.

Pushing his body onto mine, we grind against each other as if we were teenagers.

He stops for a brief moment to pull off his shirt, but then returns.

Now, we are skin to skin.

I can feel every smooth muscle with my hands

and my breasts find a home in between his strong pecs and powerful arms.

It's hard to explain the feeling you get just being under someone you love and want so much.

We are clothed below the waist and yet the nakedness above is beyond ecstatic.

It fuels my body with lust and warmth coming from somewhere deep within me.

I wrap my legs around his tight ass and press his hardness against me.

I can feel him throbbing for me, wanting me.

I can feel his passion and his desire for me and I hope he can feel mine.

"I want you," I say.

"I want you, too."

But neither of us make a move to untangle our legs.

If only there were some way to remove our pants without separating our bodies from each other's. But there isn't, so we continue just like we did before.

We move in waves.

His pelvis thrusts against mine and I respond by thrusting back.

Our arms wrap up in each other and move up and down with each wave.

Mine glide up and down his back, while his

cradle my head and neck and slowly make their way down my sides and then back up again.

"One of us has to start," I say when I can't handle the movements any longer.

I feel myself coming to the verge of pleasure and I cannot let myself get there without him inside of me.

He laughs and finally pulls away.

"Fine, fine. I'll be the strong one."

He sits up and reaches for the top of my pants.

He unbuttons the top button and then reaches down and kisses me along the edge of my panty line.

I watch as my belly button goes up and down with each breath. He pulls the top of my pants open, exposing my pelvic bone.

Then he reaches down and kisses around it, making the warm sensation deep within me rise to the surface.

I can't handle it anymore.

I push him away and step out of my clothes.

I toss my pants and underwear on the floor and then take off his.

Quickly.

Efficiently.

Without pausing for a kiss or a hello.

"Wait, wait, wait, what's the hurry?" he jokes,

trying to slow down my movements by physically pulling me up to my feet.

"I need you inside of me. Now."

I help him step out of his clothes and pull him on top of me.

He laughs and falls onto the couch.

Here we are again.

In this moment.

Alone.

He kisses my neck, and just before I close my eyes, I see that the snow is starting to gather outside.

What were only small snowflakes only half an hour ago are now thick wet flakes covering everything in sight.

The sun is no longer visible behind the curtain of gray, but we are warm and cuddled up and right where we are supposed to be.

Easton opens my legs with his and I welcome him inside.

I wrap my legs firmly around his torso and then run my hands down his strong back until I find his ass.

I grab onto it and enjoy how it flexes with each thrust.

I want to stay in this series of moments forever.

I love him, and this is the physical expression of how much.

As Easton pushes me further and further into the couch with each move, I feel our bodies becoming one.

We move as one. We breathe as one.

Suddenly, we are dancing to music that only we can hear. And then, a few moments later, a gush of emotion spills out of me.

The warmth that has been slowly building all this time, suddenly comes to the surface. My breath quickens, my chest seizes up, and my whole body suddenly quivers before a release rushes out as if it were a geyser.

I scream his name into his ear and hold on tight as his thrusts speed up and he yells mine.

Lying completely spent in his arms, I watch the snow fall.

The wind throws large flakes against the glass, but we are warm and cozy where the cold cannot hurt us.

I don't like the cold and I generally hate winters, and yet, I want to stay here forever. Glancing up at Easton, I can tell that he feels the same way.

CHAPTER 39 - EASTON

THE FOLLOWING DAY...

I've never been a big fan of Christmas growing up.

My mother would always try her best to make the day special, but my father would always find some way to mess it up.

But today, I feel different.

I open my eyes and see nothing but a blanket of snow outside the window.

It had been snowing all night, as if in preparation for the perfect Christmas morning. Bright blue sky without a cloud in sight.

I look over at Everly who is lying asleep next to me.

She is facing away from me and all I see is her long mane running down her naked body.

There's a bit of a nip in the air and I pull the thick down blanket up over her shoulders to keep her warm.

What did I ever to do in my life to be lucky enough to have her? I wonder. One thing's for sure.

I'm going to do everything in my power to make her happy.

I resist the urge to wake her up and instead watch the flurries circle outside the window. The room is warm and toasty, largely as a result of the large fireplace right in front of the bed. I've been feeding it with logs throughout the night, not letting the fire die down.

I should get some sleep, but I can't.

The thing is that I lied to Everly.

It's nothing bad, but it's pretty big.

The lie is big enough to keep me tossing and turning all night.

There's no particular reason to wait until morning except that it's Christmas and I want to do this on Christmas morning.

When I climb out of bed to tend to the fire, I hear Everly rousing behind me.

Propping herself up with her elbows, she tucks the sheet right under her armpits and looks up at me with her large doe-eyes.

Her hair falls to one side and her skin sparkles in the early morning light.

"Hey, what are you doing up so early?" she mumbles.

"I couldn't sleep."

She lies back down, curling up under the blanket.

Suddenly, I can't wait any longer.

I poke at the kindling for a moment and flip the main log on a different side to give it more oxygen.

Then I jump back in bed and under the covers with Everly.

She snuggles up her naked body next to mine and I wrap my arms around her.

"I have a question for you," I whisper into her ear. I wonder if she can hear the excitement mixed with anxiety and anticipation in my voice. Judging from the way she barely lifts her eyelids up in response, I doubt it.

Okay, now or never, I say to myself.

I sit up and reach over to the nightstand. I open the drawer and pull out a small velvet box.

Then I climb out of bed and kneel down before her on one knee.

"What are you doing?" Everly mumbles, opening her eyes a little bit.

"Everly March, I love you with all of my heart. You have given meaning to my life. You are the meaning in my life."

I can see that she is starting to realize where I am headed with this.

She sits up and wraps her arms around her knees.

She stares at me with her large eyes, her lips slightly apart in shock.

"I know that I told you that I didn't get you anything for Christmas. But that was a lie. I just couldn't wait any longer."

She shakes her head a little and pulls her shoulders up to her ears.

I flip open the velvet box, revealing the diamond ring inside.

Tears build up in the bottom of her eyes.

"Everly, I love you more than words can say. You give my life reason and you make me

want to be a better man. Everly March, will you marry me?"

She takes a moment to gather her thoughts while I wait.

My hand starts to tremble holding the velvet box open before her, but after almost a minute she reaches for it.

Suddenly, I snap it shut.

It catches her by surprise and she yelps.

"What are you doing?" Everly squeals and reaches for the box.

"You can't have this until you answer me."

I tuck the box under my arm and shake my head.

She reaches over, trying to get it but I refuse.

I pull her on top of me and she laughs. Her hair falls all over my face and I lift it up to kiss her lips.

"Will you marry me?" I ask.

She continues to laugh.

"Will you marry me? Will you marry me? Will you marry me?"

I flip her on her back and pin her body down under me.

I ask her the question over and over until she stops laughing at me and looks straight into my eyes.

"Will you marry me?" I ask one last time.

She takes a pause.

I wait.

"Yes. Of course. Of course!"

My heart beats so fast through my chest that it feels like it's about to break through. She wraps her arms around me, pressing her lips onto mine.

"Yes, yes, yes," she mumbles through the kisses. "The answer has always been yes."

* * *

As the flurries gather strength outside, we sit at the head of the bed staring at the ring that I got her.

She has placed it on her left ring finger and is staring at it in admiration. It's a big yellow center diamond with little diamonds all around.

The band is adorned with tinier diamond crystals going all the way around.

"It's the most beautiful thing I've ever seen," she whispers. "How did you know that I would like yellow?"

"I know you like the color, so I thought I'd take a chance on a canary diamond. The main stone is two-carats."

She nods, unable to take her eyes away from it.

"I'm sorry about lying to you earlier," I say after a moment.

"About what?"

"About not having a gift for you. I got this ring a long time ago, when we first got to DC."

"And you waited all this time to give it to me?"

"I wanted it all to be over. I wanted to ask when all of that was behind us."

"And if it wasn't?"

"Well, then maybe I would've proposed anyway."

Everly gives me a small nod.

"You're forgiven," she whispers.

CHAPTER 40 - EVERLY

IT'S ONLY THE BEGINNING...

Snow is blowing in all directions when Easton parks the car in the lonely lot.

It's noon, but the day is so gray and bleak that I doubt that we will see even a ray of light today.

"Are you sure you want to do this?" he asks, taking my hand in his.

By the tone of his voice, I can tell that he's not having second thoughts.

He is excited and committed; he just doesn't want me to have any doubts. I don't.

"Yes, I do."

"Are you sure?" he asks.

The second time he asks, I suddenly start to wonder.

What if he is having doubts.

"Do you?" I ask, pulling my hand away.

"Yes, of course," he says quickly. "I just know that this grayness isn't your favorite. And just because it seemed like a good idea yesterday doesn't mean that we have to commit to it. We have our whole lives to do this. So if you want something else for your wedding day, I totally understand."

I look out of the window at the white snowflakes beating against the side window. The weather outside isn't exactly ideal.

That's true.

But so what?

I've spent a lot of time in a tropical paradise and the reality of that place was far from perfect.

My heart skips a beat.

And then it skips another.

"I want to marry you," I say, turning to him.

"I know. I do, too. I'm just saying that if this isn't what you imagined your wedding to be, we can totally wait and have something a bit more...grand."

I look out of the window at the courthouse.

It doesn't look like much.

There are no columns and there are no steps leading up to the top. In fact, it's just a one-story municipal building with very few frills.

"This place is...perfect," I say. "Don't get me

wrong, it's nothing like what I expected my wedding to be and that's exactly what makes it so right. We already had a chance at ostentation and grandeur and a big lavish affair. And our wedding there would've been all wrong."

He nods and gives me a kiss on the lips. Then he turns off the engine.

"Shall we?"

* * *

A FEW MINUTES LATER, we are standing facing each other before the Justice of the Peace. I am dressed in tight-fitting dark jeans and boots and a white fluffy seater with a V-neck.

It's the most wedding themed attire I had on a moment's notice.

Easton is wearing a jacket with a collared shirt and dark pants.

The room is illuminated by bright fluorescent lights and it looks like my sixth-grade classroom without all the wall decorations.

Low ceiling.

A few windows.

Linoleum floor that squeaks under my feet.

This place is the least romantic place in the

world except for one thing...this is the place where I am going to become his wife.

The Justice of the Peace asks Easton to repeat his words.

He looks deep into my eyes and gives me a little wink.

"I, Easton Bay, take you, Everly March, to be my lawful wife, to have and to hold from this day forward, for better, for worse, for richer or for poorer, in sickness and in health while we both shall live."

My chest seizes up and I can't take a full breath.

Fighting back tears, I promise Easton the same thing he just promised me.

"I now pronounce you husband and wife. You may now kiss."

Easton pulls me into his arms and presses his lips onto mine.

I close my eyes and lose myself in the moment.

We have kissed a million times before, but this feels like the first time.

WHEN WE GET BACK to the car, we can't stop smiling.

"I love you so much, Everly."

"I love you, too. I can't wait to get back to our cabin and curl up in front of the fire and not leave for a long, long time."

He starts the car and pulls out of the parking lot.

"Oh, no, I just remembered," I say. "We only have the place until tomorrow. That's a...bummer."

"Actually, I extended our stay for a month. So, if you want, we can get home, climb under the covers, and not leave until the end of January."

"I like that."

Whatever guilt I felt earlier about not inviting anyone to our wedding has dissipated completely.

That moment felt right and true and it will stay with me forever. It doesn't matter that no one else was there.

It doesn't matter that it happened in the dead of winter and I didn't even hold a flower in my hand.

It doesn't matter that I wasn't wearing a dress, let alone a white dress or a wedding gown.

Easton is my husband and I am his wife.

THANK you for reading THRONE OF YORK! I hope you enjoyed the conclusion of Everly and Easton's story.

If you enjoyed this series, I know you will LOVE my new book. **One-click TANGLED UP IN ICE now!**

I am the recluse billionaire of New York.

Holed up in a twelve thousand square foot mansion overlooking Central Park, I spend my days doing the only thing I was ever good at: making money.

Not long ago, I had everything a man could want. But then in one moment I lost everything that mattered.

In the middle of the most bustling metropolis in the world, I've managed to live my life completely isolated from society for almost four years.

But then she came along.

Disheveled. Lost. Innocent.

She crashed into my perfect tucked away life and changed *everything*.

One-click TANGLED UP IN ICE now!

Sign up for my newsletter to find out when I have new books!

You can also join my Facebook group, **Charlotte Byrd's Reader Club**, for exclusive giveaways and sneak peaks of future books.

I appreciate you sharing my books and telling your friends about them. Reviews help readers find my books! Please leave a review on your favorite site.

READ the sneak peak of Tangled Up in Ice on the following page!

PROLOGUE

Her small, delicate mouth parts in the middle.

She licks her lower lip and my body burns for hers. I lift my chin to hers. Our lips collide.

I bury my hands in her hair.

It's soft and damp with an earthy scent that doesn't come from any shampoo bottle.

She is soft and snug in my arms and she pulls away only far enough to utter, "I love you, too."

I clutch her closer, wrapping her arms around mind.

Her breaths become mine and mine become hers.

Her hands are ice.

She slips them under my shirt and my back recoils for a moment before welcoming her in.

I'm restless and hungry for her.

All of her.

Right now.

That's what she does to me.

One touch and I have to have her.

Another touch and I morph into a beast who can't control his impulses.

With her chin tilted toward the ceiling, her long hair moves in waves.

I run my hands down the contours of her body. I know every curve and every dip.

The more I feel, the greedier I become.

CHAPTER 1 - JACKSON

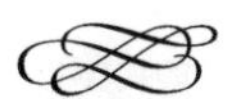

HATE

I hate this city.

I hate the grime.

I hate the sad and angry faces that people make as they walk down the sidewalk.

I hate the rush.

I hate that everyone has somewhere more important to be than the person next to them.

I hate the way the poor kids from the projects look at rich kids with personal drivers.

And I hate the way kids with drivers look at everyone else, like they are specks of dirt beneath their feet.

I hate that a family of five has to cram into a one-bedroom apartment and pay two-thirds of their income in rent for the luxury of a two hours commute.

I hate that I live alone in twelve thousand square foot, five-story mansion with a view of Central Park from practically every window.

I hate the summers with their hoards of tourists taking pictures of every mundane and uninteresting thing.

I hate the fall and the spring, with its torrential rains which chill you to the bone and make the city grey and gloomy for weeks.

But most of all, I hate those five weeks between Thanksgiving and New Year that everyone else seems to find so magical.

It's the time of year that people spend hours gawking at window displays designed to dazzle and make you forget that you really can't afford anything there.

I hate the blinding lights that twinkle all day and all night without a moment's peace. But mostly I hate the cheer that fills the city, which only has one real purpose - to sell more crap.

I hate people and I hate that I'm all alone.

I hate that I haven't left this house in almost four years and I hate how much I like being alone.

I hate that all I do is work, but without work, I'd have even less than I do now.

I hate my money, and I hate to imagine a world in which I don't have it.

But mostly I hate myself.

I hate the scars that cover my body.

I hate that every time I look at them, my mind is flooded with memories of *that* day.

I hate that the person I used to be is gone and I hate that I can't imagine my life without all of this hate.

CHAPTER 2 - HARLEY

LOVE

I love this city.

I love the traffic jams, people honking when they are standing still with absolutely nowhere to go.

I love the lights that illuminate the streets until twilight.

I love that something is always going on.

I love that everyone is always in a hurry.

Where are they going?

What are they doing?

What is it that's so important?

I love how hot and steamy and unbearable the summers get.

I love how everyone who has anywhere to go takes off for the Hamptons, Connecticut, Vermont, leaving the the rest of us with a bit more room to stretch out.

The summers bring in all the tourists and I even love them.

I was one of those tourists once.

When I turned fourteen, my parents took me here to show me the sights.

The Statue of Liberty.

Broadway.

Times Square.

The typical places that all real New Yorkers avoid.

That's when I first fell in love with the city, and that's when I knew that I had to do everything in my power to move here.

And the thing that I love most is that magical time between Thanksgiving and New Year's.

The tree lighting ceremony in Rockefeller Center.

Ice skating in Central Park.

The store fronts and the lights that seem to explode in life.

But I also love this city on those other less lovable days: the cold, slushy days of February that are all too short.

I love the dirty snow that appears a day after a

big blizzard, and I love the way there's always one rebel pizza place that remains open while the rest of the city closes down and everyone crams into it for a bite.

I love the lights.

I love the crowds.

I even love my apartment.

And that's not easy to love.

It's a four-hundred square foot studio and I share it with a roommate.

Yet, I still love it.

I love the tiny kitchen in which every appliance is miniature.

I love the little closet which only fits half of my clothes and I don't even shop that much.

I love the little bathroom that has no space around the sink for clutter. I house the shampoo and conditioner in a wire hanger around the shower, keeping the rest of the products in boxes under the bed.

Why do I love this apartment?

I can't help it.

It's about the size of a large Barbie Dream House if she had a Dream New York Apartment, but it's enough for me.

Maybe there's something more to all of this?

Maybe I love this place because of how it makes me feel about myself.

Despite what I have or rather don't have, I feel important.

Special.

New York does that to people to get them to move here.

It's almost as if the city itself sends you these subliminal messages that say no matter how crappy your apartment is or how crowded and loud and angry people, you're in New York.

And being here is enough.

That has to true, right? Why would I love this place otherwise?

Can't wait read more? One-click TANGLED UP IN ICE now!

BLACK EDGE

Want to read a "Decadent, delicious, & dangerously addictive!" romance you will not be able to put down? The entire series is out! **1-Click Black Edge NOW!**

I don't belong here.

I'm in way over my head. But I have debts to pay.

They call my name. The spotlight is on. The auction starts.

Mr. Black is the highest bidder. He's dark, rich, and powerful. He likes to play games.

The only rule is there are no rules.

But it's just one night. **What's the worst that can happen?**

1-Click BLACK EDGE Now!

* * *

START READING BLACK EDGE ON THE NEXT PAGE!

CHAPTER 1- ELLIE

WHEN THE INVITATION ARRIVES...

"Here it is! Here it is!" my roommate Caroline yells at the top of her lungs as she runs into my room.

We were friends all through Yale and we moved to New York together after graduation.

Even though I've known Caroline for what feels like a million years, I am still shocked by the exuberance of her voice. It's quite loud given the smallness of her body.

Caroline is one of those super skinny girls who can eat pretty much anything without gaining a pound.

Unfortunately, I am not that talented. In fact, my body seems to have the opposite gift. I can eat nothing but vegetables for a week straight, eat one slice of pizza, and gain a pound.

"What is it?" I ask, forcing myself to sit up.

It's noon and I'm still in bed.

My mother thinks I'm depressed and wants me to see her shrink.

She might be right, but I can't fathom the strength.

"The invitation!" Caroline says jumping in bed next to me.

I stare at her blankly.

And then suddenly it hits me.

This must be *the* invitation.

"You mean...it's..."

"Yes!" she screams and hugs me with excitement.

"Oh my God!" She gasps for air and pulls away from me almost as quickly.

"Hey, you know I didn't brush my teeth yet," I say turning my face away from hers.

"Well, what are you waiting for? Go brush them," she instructs.

Begrudgingly, I make my way to the bathroom.

We have been waiting for this invitation for some time now.

And by we, I mean Caroline.

I've just been playing along, pretending to care, not really expecting it to show up.

Without being able to contain her excitement, Caroline bursts through the door when my mouth is still full of toothpaste.

She's jumping up and down, holding a box in her hand.

"Wait, what's that?" I mumble and wash my mouth out with water.

"This is it!" Caroline screeches and pulls me into the living room before I have a chance to wipe my mouth with a towel.

"But it's a box," I say staring at her.

"Okay, okay," Caroline takes a couple of deep yoga breaths, exhaling loudly.

She puts the box carefully on our dining room table. There's no address on it.

It looks something like a fancy gift box with a big monogrammed C in the middle.

Is the C for Caroline?

"Is this how it came? There's no address on it?" I ask.

"It was hand-delivered," Caroline whispers.

I hold my breath as she carefully removes the top part, revealing the satin and silk covered wood box inside.

The top of it is gold plated with whimsical twirls all around the edges, and the mirrored area is engraved with her full name.

Caroline Elizabeth Kennedy Spruce.

Underneath her name is a date, one week in the future. 8 PM.

We stare at it for a few moments until Caroline reaches for the elegant knob to open the box.

Inside, Caroline finds a custom monogram made of foil in gold on silk emblazoned on the inside of the flap cover.

There's also a folio covered in silk. Caroline carefully opens the folio and finds another foil monogram and the invitation.

The inside invitation is one layer, shimmer white, with gold writing.

"Is this for real? How many layers of invitation are there?" I ask.

But the presentation is definitely doing its job. We are both duly impressed.

"There's another knob," I say, pointing to the knob in front of the box.

I'm not sure how we had missed it before.

Caroline carefully pulls on this knob, revealing a drawer that holds the inserts (a card with directions and a response card).

"Oh my God, I can't go to this alone," Caroline mumbles, turning to me.

I stare blankly at her.

Getting invited to this party has been her dream ever since she found out about it from someone in the Cicada 17, a super-secret society at Yale.

"Look, here, it says that I can bring a friend," she yells out even though I'm standing right next to her.

"It probably says a date. A plus one?" I say.

"No, a friend. Girl preferred," Caroline reads off the invitation card.

That part of the invitation is in very small ink, as if someone made the person stick it on, without their express permission.

"I don't want to crash," I say.

Frankly, I don't really want to go.

These kind of upper-class events always make me feel a little bit uncomfortable.

"Hey, aren't you supposed to be at work?" I ask.

"Eh, I took a day off," Caroline says waving her arm. "I knew that the invitation would come today and I just couldn't deal with work. You know how it is."

I nod. Sort of.

Caroline and I seem like we come from the same world.

We both graduated from private school, we both went to Yale, and our parents belong to the same exclusive country club in Greenwich, Connecticut.

But we're not really that alike.

Caroline's family has had money for many generations going back to the railroads.

My parents were an average middle class family from Connecticut.

They were both teachers and our idea of summering was renting a 1-bedroom bungalow near Clearwater, FL for a week.

But then my parents got divorced when I was 8, and my mother started tutoring kids to make extra money.

The pay was the best in Greenwich, where parents paid more than $100 an hour.

And that's how she met, Mitch Willoughby, my stepfather.

He was a widower with a five-year old daughter who was not doing well after her mom's untimely death.

Even though Mom didn't usually tutor anyone younger than 12, she agreed to take a meeting with Mitch and his daughter because $200 an hour was too much to turn down.

Three months later, they were in love and six

months later, he asked her to marry him on top of the Eiffel Tower.

They got married, when I was 11, in a huge 450-person ceremony in Nantucket.

So even though Caroline and I run in the same circles, we're not really from the same circle.

It has nothing to do with her, she's totally accepting, it's me.

I don't always feel like I belong.

Caroline majored in art-history at Yale, and she now works at an exclusive contemporary art gallery in Soho.

It's chic and tiny, featuring only 3 pieces of art at a time.

Ash, the owner - I'm not sure if that's her first or last name - mainly keeps the space as a showcase. What the gallery really specializes in is going to wealthy people's homes and choosing their art for them.

They're basically interior designers, but only for art.

None of the pieces sell for anything less than $200 grand, but Caroline's take home salary is about $21,000.

Clearly, not enough to pay for our 2 bedroom apartment in Chelsea.

Her parents cover her part of the rent and pay all of her other expenses.

Mine do too, of course.

Well, Mitch does.

I only make about $27,000 at my writer's assistant job and that's obviously not covering my half of our $6,000 per month apartment.

So, what's the difference between me and Caroline?

I guess the only difference is that I feel bad about taking the money.

I have a $150,000 school loan from Yale that I don't want Mitch to pay for.

It's my loan and I'm going to pay for it myself, dammit.

Plus, unlike Caroline, I know that real people don't really live like this.

Real people like my dad, who is being pressured to sell the house for more than a million dollars that he and my mom bought back in the late 80's (the neighborhood has gone up in price and teachers now have to make way for tech entrepreneurs and real estate moguls).

"How can you just not go to work like that? Didn't you use all of your sick days flying to Costa Rica last month?" I ask.

"Eh, who cares? Ash totally understands. Besides, she totally owes me. If it weren't for me, she would've never closed that geek millionaire who had the hots for me and ended up buying close to a million dollars' worth of art for his new mansion."

Caroline does have a way with men.

She's fun and outgoing and perky.

The trick, she once told me, is to figure out exactly what the guy wants to hear.

Because a geek millionaire, as she calls anyone who has made money in tech, does not want to hear the same thing that a football player wants to hear.

And neither of them want to hear what a trust fund playboy wants to hear.

But Caroline isn't a gold digger.

Not at all.

Her family owns half the East Coast.

And when it comes to men, she just likes to have fun.

I look at the time.

It's my day off, but that doesn't mean that I want to spend it in bed in my pajamas, listening to Caroline obsessing over what she's going to wear.

No, today, is my day to actually get some writing done.

I'm going to Starbucks, getting a table in the

back, near the bathroom, and am actually going to finish this short story that I've been working on for a month.

Or maybe start a new one.

I go to my room and start getting dressed.

I have to wear something comfortable, but something that's not exactly work clothes.

I hate how all of my clothes have suddenly become work clothes. It's like they've been tainted.

They remind me of work and I can't wear them out anymore on any other occasion. I'm not a big fan of my work, if you can't tell.

Caroline follows me into my room and plops down on my bed.

I take off my pajamas and pull on a pair of leggings.

Ever since these have become the trend, I find myself struggling to force myself into a pair of jeans.

They're just so comfortable!

"Okay, I've come to a decision," Caroline says. "You *have* to come with me!"

"Oh, I have to come with you?" I ask, incredulously. "Yeah, no, I don't think so."

"Oh c'mon! Please! Pretty please! It will be so much fun!"

"Actually, you can't make any of those promises.

You have no idea what it will be," I say, putting on a long sleeve shirt and a sweater with a zipper in the front.

Layers are important during this time of year.

The leaves are changing colors, winds are picking up, and you never know if it's going to be one of those gorgeous warm, crisp New York days they like to feature in all those romantic comedies or a soggy, overcast dreary day that only shows up in one scene at the end when the two main characters fight or break up (but before they get back together again).

"Okay, yes, I see your point," Caroline says, sitting up and crossing her legs. "But here is what we *do* know. We do know that it's going to be amazing. I mean, look at the invitation. It's a freakin' box with engravings and everything!"

Usually, Caroline is much more eloquent and better at expressing herself.

"Okay, yes, the invitation is impressive," I admit.

"And as you know, the invitation is everything. I mean, it really sets the mood for the party. The event! And not just the mood. It establishes a certain expectation. And this box..."

"Yes, the invitation definitely sets up a certain expectation," I agree.

"So?"

"So?" I ask her back.

"Don't you want to find out what that expectation is?"

"No." I shake my head categorically.

"Okay. So what else do we know?" Caroline asks rhetorically as I pack away my Mac into my bag.

"I have to go, Caroline," I say.

"No, listen. The yacht. Of course, the yacht. How could I bury the lead like that?" She jumps up and down with excitement again.

"We also know that it's going to be this super exclusive event on a *yacht*! And not just some small 100 footer, but a *mega*-yacht."

I stare at her blankly, pretending to not be impressed.

When Caroline first found out about this party, through her ex-boyfriend, we spent days trying to figure out what made this event so special.

But given that neither of us have been on a yacht before, at least not a mega-yacht – we couldn't quite get it.

"You know the yacht is going to be amazing!"

"Yes, of course," I give in. "But that's why I'm sure that you're going to have a wonderful time by yourself. I have to go."

I grab my keys and toss them into the bag.

"Ellie," Caroline says.

The tone of her voice suddenly gets very serious, to match the grave expression on her face.

"Ellie, please. I don't think I can go by myself."

CHAPTER 2 - ELLIE

WHEN YOU HAVE COFFEE WITH A GUY YOU CAN'T HAVE...

And that's pretty much how I was roped into going.

You don't know Caroline, but if you did, the first thing you'd find out is that she is not one to take things seriously.

Nothing fazes her.

Nothing worries her.

Sometimes she is the most enlightened person on earth, other times she's the densest.

Most of the time, I'm jealous of the fact that she simply lives life in the present.

"So, you're going?" my friend Tom asks.

He brought me my pumpkin spice latte, the first one of the season!

I close my eyes and inhale it's sweet aroma before taking the first sip.

But even before its wonderful taste of cinnamon and nutmeg runs down my throat, Tom is already criticizing my decision.

"I can't believe you're actually going," he says.

"Oh my God, now I know it's officially fall," I change the subject.

"Was there actually such a thing as autumn before the pumpkin spice latte? I mean, I remember that we had falling leaves, changing colors, all that jazz, but without this...it's like Christmas without a Christmas tree."

"Ellie, it's a day after Labor Day," Tom rolls his eyes. "It's not fall yet."

I take another sip. "Oh yes, I do believe it is."

"Stop changing the subject," Tom takes a sip of his plain black coffee.

How he doesn't get bored with that thing, I'll never know.

But that's the thing about Tom.

He's reliable.

Always on time, never late.

It's nice. That's what I have always liked about him.

He's basically the opposite of Caroline in every way.

And that's what makes seeing him like this, as only a friend, so hard.

"Why are you going there? Can't Caroline go by herself?" Tom asks, looking straight into my eyes.

His hair has this annoying tendency of falling into his face just as he's making a point – as a way of accentuating it.

It's actually quite vexing especially given how irresistible it makes him look.

His eyes twinkle under the low light in the back of the Starbucks.

"I'm going as her plus one," I announce.

I make my voice extra perky on purpose.

So that it portrays excitement, rather than apprehensiveness, which is actually how I'm feeling over the whole thing.

"She's making you go as her plus one," Tom announces as a matter a fact. He knows me too well.

"I just don't get it, Ellie. I mean, why bother? It's a super yacht filled with filthy rich people. I mean, how fun can that party be?"

"Jealous much?" I ask.

"I'm not jealous at all!" He jumps back in his seat. "If that's what you think..."

He lets his words trail off and suddenly the conversation takes on a more serious mood.

"You don't have to worry, I'm not going to miss your engagement party," I say quietly. It's the weekend after I get back."

He shakes his head and insists that that's not what he's worried about.

"I just don't get it Ellie," he says.

You don't get it?

You don't get why I'm going?

I've had feelings for you for, what, two years now?

But the time was never right.

At first, I was with my boyfriend and the night of our breakup, you decided to kiss me.

You totally caught me off guard.

And after that long painful breakup, I wasn't ready for a relationship.

And you, my best friend, you weren't really a rebound contender.

And then, just as I was about to tell you how I felt, you spend the night with Carrie.

Beautiful, wealthy, witty Carrie. Carrie Warrenhouse, the current editor of BuzzPost, the online magazine where we both work, and the daughter of Edward Warrenhouse, the owner of BuzzPost.

Oh yeah, and on top of all that, you also started seeing her and then asked her to marry you.

And now you two are getting married on Valentine's Day.

And I'm really happy for you.

Really.

Truly.

The only problem is that I'm also in love with you.

And now, I don't know what the hell to do with all of this except get away from New York.

Even if it's just for a few days.

But of course, I can't say any of these things.

Especially the last part.

"This hasn't been the best summer," I say after a few moments. "And I just want to do something fun. Get out of town. Go to a party. Because that's all this is, a party."

"That's not what I heard," Tom says.

"What do you mean?"

"Ever since you told me you were going, I started looking into this event.

And the rumor is that it's not what it is."

I shake my head, roll my eyes.

"What? You don't believe me?" Tom asks incredulously.

I shake my head.

"Okay, what? What did you hear?"

"It's basically like a Playboy Mansion party on steroids. It's totally out of control. Like one big orgy."

"And you would know what a Playboy Mansion party is like," I joke.

"I'm being serious, Ellie. I'm not sure this is a good place for you. I mean, you're not Caroline."

"And what the hell does that mean?" I ask.

Now, I'm actually insulted.

At first, I was just listening because I thought he was being protective.

But now...

"What you don't think I'm fun enough? You don't think I like to have a good time?" I ask.

"That's not what I meant," Tom backtracks. I start to gather my stuff. "What are you doing?"

"No, you know what," I stop packing up my stuff. "I'm not leaving. You're leaving."

"Why?"

"Because I came here to write. I have work to do. I staked out this table and I'm not leaving until I have something written. I thought you wanted to have coffee with me. I thought we were friends. I didn't realize that you came here to chastise me about my decisions."

"That's not what I'm doing," Tom says, without getting out of his chair.

"You have to leave Tom. I want you to leave."

"I just don't understand what happened to us," he says getting up, reluctantly.

I stare at him as if he has lost his mind.

"You have no right to tell me what I can or can't do. You don't even have the right to tell your fiancée. Unless you don't want her to stay your fiancée for long."

"I'm not trying to tell you what to do, Ellie. I'm just worried. This super exclusive party on some mega-yacht, that's not you. That's not us."

"Not us? You've got to be kidding," I shake my head. "You graduated from Princeton, Tom. Your father is an attorney at one of the most prestigious law-firms in Boston. He has argued cases before the Supreme Court. You're going to marry the heir to the Warrenhouse fortune. I'm so sick and tired of your working class hero attitude, I can't even tell you. Now, are you going to leave or should I?"

The disappointment that I saw in Tom's eyes hurt me to my very soul.

But he had hurt me.

His engagement came completely out of left field.

I had asked him to give me some time after my breakup and after waiting for only two months, he started dating Carrie.

And then they moved in together. And then he asked her to marry him.

And throughout all that, he just sort of pretended that we were still friends.

Just like none of this ever happened.

I open my computer and stare at the half written story before me.

Earlier today, before Caroline, before Tom, I had all of these ideas.

I just couldn't wait to get started.

But now...I doubted that I could even spell my name right.

Staring at a non-moving blinker never fuels the writing juices.

I close my computer and look around the place.

All around me, people are laughing and talking.

Leggings and Uggs are back in season – even though the days are still warm and crispy.

It hasn't rained in close to a week and everyone's

good mood seems to be energized by the bright rays of the afternoon sun.

Last spring, I was certain that Tom and I would get together over the summer and I would spend the fall falling in love with my best friend.

And now?

Now, he's engaged to someone else.

Not just someone else – my boss!

And we just had a fight over some stupid party that I don't even really want to go to.

He's right, of course.

It's not my style.

My family might have money, but that's not the world in which I'm comfortable.

I'm always standing on the sidelines and it's not going to be any different at this party.

But if I don't go now, after this, that means that I'm listening to him.

And he has no right to tell me what to do.

So, I have to go.

How did everything get so messed up?

CHAPTER 3 - ELLIE

WHEN YOU GO SHOPPING FOR THE PARTY OF A LIFETIME...

"What the hell are you still doing hanging out with that asshole?" Caroline asks dismissively.

We are in Elle's, a small boutique in Soho, where you can shop by appointment only.

I didn't even know these places existed until Caroline introduced me to the concept.

Caroline is not a fan of Tom.

They never got along, not since he called her an East Side snob at our junior year Christmas party at Yale and she called him a middle class poseur.

Neither insult was very creative, but their insults got better over the years as their hatred for each other grew.

You know how in the movies, two characters who

hate each other in the beginning always end up falling in love by the end?

Well, for a while, I actually thought that would happen to them.

If not fall in love, at least hook up. But no, they stayed steadfast in their hatred.

"That guy is such a tool. I mean, who the hell is he to tell you what to do anyway? It's not like you're his girlfriend," Caroline says placing a silver beaded bandage dress to her body and extending her right leg in front.

Caroline is definitely a knock out.

She's 5'10", 125 pounds with legs that go up to her chin.

In fact, from far away, she seems to be all blonde hair and legs and nothing else.

"I think he was just concerned, given all the stuff that is out there about this party."

"Okay, first of all, you have to stop calling it a party."

"Why? What is it?"

"It's not a party. It's like calling a wedding a party. Is it a party? Yes. But is it bigger than that."

"I had no idea that you were so sensitive to language. Fine. What do you want me to call it?'

"An experience," she announces, completely seriously.

"Are you kidding me? No way. There's no way I'm going to call it an experience."

We browse in silence for a few moments.

Some of the dresses and tops and shoes are pretty, some aren't.

I'm the first to admit that I do not have the vocabulary or knowledge to appreciate a place like this.

Now, Caroline on the other hand...

"Oh my God, I'm just in love with all these one of a kind pieces you have here," she says to the woman upfront who immediately starts to beam with pride.

"That's what we're going for."

"These statement bags and the detailing on these booties – agh! To die for, right?" Caroline says and they both turn to me.

"Yeah, totally," I agree blindly.

"And these high-end core pieces, I could just wear this every day!" Caroline pulls up a rather structured cream colored short sleeve shirt with a tassel hem and a boxy fit.

I'm not sure what makes that shirt a so-called core piece, but I go with the flow.

I'm out of my element and I know it.

"Okay, so what are we supposed to wear to this *experience* if we don't even know what's going to be going on there."

"I'm not exactly sure but definitely not jeans and t-shirts," Caroline says referring to my staple outfit. "But the invitation also said not to worry. They have all the necessities if we forget something."

As I continue to aimlessly browse, my mind starts to wander.

And goes back to Tom.

I met Tom at the Harvard-Yale game.

He was my roommate's boyfriend's high school best friend and he came up for the weekend to visit him.

We became friends immediately.

One smile from him, even on Skype, made all of my worries disappear.

He just sort of got me, the way no one really did.

After graduation, we applied to work a million different online magazines and news outlets, but BuzzPost was the one place that took both of us.

We didn't exactly plan to end up at the same place, but it was a nice coincidence.

He even asked if I wanted to be his roommate – but I had already agreed to room with Caroline.

He ended up in this crappy fourth floor walkup

in Hell's Kitchen – one of the only buildings that they haven't gentrified yet.

So, the rent was still somewhat affordable. Like I said, Tom likes to think of himself as a working class hero even though his upbringing is far from it.

Whenever he came over to our place, he always made fun of how expensive the place was, but it was always in good fun.

At least, it felt like it at the time.

Now?

I'm not so sure anymore.

"Do you think that Tom is really going to get married?" I ask Caroline while we're changing.

She swings my curtain open in front of the whole store.

I'm topless, but luckily I'm facing away from her and the assistant is buried in her phone.

"What are you doing?" I shriek and pull the curtain closed.

"What are you thinking?" she demands.

I manage to grab a shirt and cover myself before Caroline pulls the curtain open again.

She is standing before me in only a bra and a matching pair of panties – completely confident and unapologetic.

I think she's my spirit animal.

"Who cares about Tom?" Caroline demands.

"I do," I say meekly.

"Well, you shouldn't. He's a dick. You are way too good for him. I don't even understand what you see in him."

"He's my friend," I say as if that explains everything.

Caroline knows how long I've been in love with Tom.

She knows everything.

At times, I wish I hadn't been so open.

But other times, it's nice to have someone to talk to.

Even if she isn't exactly understanding.

"You can't just go around pining for him, Ellie. You can do so much better than him. You were with your ex and he just hung around waiting and waiting. Never telling you how he felt. Never making any grand gestures."

Caroline is big on gestures.

The grander the better.

She watches a lot of movies and she demands them of her dates.

And the funny thing is that you often get exactly what you ask from the world.

"I don't care about that," I say. "We were in the wrong place for each other.

I was with someone and then I wasn't ready to jump into another relationship right away.

And then...he and Carrie got together."

"There's no such thing as not the right time. Life is what you make it, Ellie. You're in control of your life. And I hate the fact that you're acting like you're not the main character in your own movie."

"I don't even know what you're talking about," I say.

"All I'm saying is that you deserve someone who tells you how he feels. Someone who isn't afraid of rejection. Someone who isn't afraid to put it all out there."

"Maybe that's who you want," I say.

"And that's not who you want?" Caroline says taking a step back away from me.

I think about it for a moment.

"Well, no I wouldn't say that. It is who I want," I finally say. "But I had a boyfriend then. And Tom and I were friends. So I couldn't expect him to—"

"You couldn't expect him to put it all out there? Tell you how he feels and take the risk of getting hurt?" Caroline cuts me off.

I hate to admit it, but that's exactly what I want.

That's exactly what I wanted from him back then.

I didn't want him to just hang around being my friend, making me question my feelings for him.

And if he had done that, if he had told me how he felt about me earlier, before my awful breakup, then I would've jumped in.

I would've broken up with my ex immediately to be with him.

"So, is that what I should do now? Now that things are sort of reversed?" I ask.

"What do you mean?"

"I mean, now that he's the one in the relationship. Should I just put it all out there? Tell him how I feel. Leave it all on the table, so to speak."

Caroline takes a moment to think about this.

I appreciate it because I know how little she thinks of him.

"Because I don't know if I can," I add quietly.

"Maybe that's your answer right there," Caroline finally says. "If you did want him, really want him to be yours, then you wouldn't be able to not to. You'd have to tell him."

I go back into my dressing room and pull the curtain closed.

I look at myself in the mirror.

The pale girl with green eyes and long dark hair is a coward.

She is afraid of life.

Afraid to really live.

Would this ever change?

CHAPTER 4 - ELLIE

WHEN YOU DECIDE TO LIVE YOUR LIFE...

"Are you ready?" Caroline bursts into my room. "Our cab is downstairs."

No, I'm not ready.

Not at all.

But I'm going.

I take one last look in the mirror and grab my suitcase.

As the cab driver loads our bags into the trunk, Caroline takes my hand, giddy with excitement.

Excited is not how I would describe my state of being.

More like reluctant.

And terrified.

When I get into the cab, my stomach drops and I feel like I'm going to throw up.

But then the feeling passes.

"I can't believe this is actually happening," I say.

"I know, right? I'm so happy you're doing this with me, Ellie. I mean, really. I don't know if I could go by myself."

After ten minutes of meandering through the convoluted streets of lower Manhattan, the cab drops us off in front of a nondescript office building.

"Is the party here?" I ask.

Caroline shakes her head with a little smile on her face.

She knows something I don't know.

I can tell by that mischievous look on her face.

"What's going on?" I ask.

But she doesn't give in.

Instead, she just nudges me inside toward the security guard at the front desk.

She hands him a card, he nods, and shows us to the elevator.

"Top floor," he says.

When we reach the top floor, the elevator doors swing open on the roof and a strong gust of wind knocks into me.

Out of the corner of my eye, I see it.

The helicopter.

The blades are already going.

A man approaches us and takes our bags.

"What are we doing here?" I yell on top of my lungs.

But Caroline doesn't hear me.

I follow her inside the helicopter, ducking my head to make sure that I get in all in one piece.

A few minutes later, we take off.

We fly high above Manhattan, maneuvering past the buildings as if we're birds.

I've never been in a helicopter before and, a part of me, wishes that I'd had some time to process this beforehand.

"I didn't tell you because I thought you would freak," Caroline says into her headset.

She knows me too well.

She pulls out her phone and we pose for a few selfies.

"It's beautiful up here," I say looking out the window.

In the afternoon sun, the Manhattan skyline is breathtaking.

The yellowish red glow bounces off the glass buildings and shimmers in the twilight.

I don't know where we are going, but for the first time in a long time, I don't care.

I stay in the moment and enjoy it for everything it's worth.

Quickly the skyscrapers and the endless parade of bridges disappear and all that remains below us is the glistening of the deep blue sea.

And then suddenly, somewhere in the distance I see it.

The yacht.

At first, it appears as barely a speck on the horizon.

But as we fly closer, it grows in size.

By the time we land, it seems to be the size of its own island.

A TALL, beautiful woman waves to us as we get off the helicopter.

She's holding a plate with glasses of champagne and nods to a man in a tuxedo next to her to take our bags.

"Wow, that was quite an entrance," Caroline says to me.

"Mr. Black knows how to welcome his guests,"

the woman says. "My name is Lizbeth and I am here to serve you."

Lizbeth shows us around the yacht and to our stateroom.

"There will be cocktails right outside when you're ready," Lizbeth said before leaving us alone.

As soon as she left, we grabbed hands and let out a big yelp.

"Oh my God! Can you believe this place?" Caroline asks.

"No, it's amazing," I say, running over to the balcony. The blueness of the ocean stretched out as far as the eye could see.

"Are you going to change for cocktails?" Caroline asks, sitting down at the vanity. "The helicopter did a number on my hair."

We both crack up laughing.

Neither of us have ever been on a helicopter before – let alone a boat this big.

I decide against a change of clothes – my Nordstrom leggings and polka dot blouse should do just fine for cocktail hour.

But I do slip off my pair of flats and put on a nice pair of pumps, to dress up the outfit a little bit.

While Caroline changes into her short black

dress, I brush the tangles out of my hair and reapply my lipstick.

"Ready?" Caroline asks.

Can't wait to read more? **One-Click BLACK EDGE Now!**

ABOUT CHARLOTTE BYRD

Charlotte Byrd is the bestselling author of many contemporary romance novels. She lives in Southern California with her husband, son, and a crazy toy Australian Shepherd. She loves books, hot weather and crystal blue waters.

Write her here:

charlotte@charlotte-byrd.com

Check out her books here:

www.charlotte-byrd.com

Connect with her here:

www.facebook.com/charlottebyrdbooks

Instagram: @charlottebyrdbooks

Twitter: @ByrdAuthor

Facebook Group: Charlotte Byrd's Reader Club

Newsletter

Made in the USA
Middletown, DE
07 August 2020